SUPERLOO: KING TUT'S GOLDEN TOILET

W. C. Flushing

Illustrated by Martin Chatterton

First published in 2006 by
Puffin Books
This Large Print edition published by
BBC Audiobooks
by arrangement with
Penguin Books Ltd 2008

ISBN: 978 1405 662451

British Library Cataloguing in Publication Data available

Printed and bound in Great Britain by
Antony Rowe Ltd., Chippenham, Wiltshire

CHAPTER ONE

Finn was being chased. The boy chasing him was wearing a black top with the hood up. Finn couldn't see his face. But he could see that the boy was bigger than him. And that even if Finn was a fast runner, which he wasn't, this boy would be much faster because he was on Rollerblades.

He'd come swooping out of nowhere.

'Hey,' he'd yelled. 'Kid in the orange T-shirt. I want to talk to you!'

Finn hadn't reacted at first. He'd just

felt sorry for that kid in the orange T-shirt. Whoever he was, he was in deep trouble. Then he'd looked down. And his stomach did a sick flip. His heart went into overdrive.

'It's me.'

He'd forgotten—in his desperate rush to get out of the house that morning, he'd grabbed the first T-shirt he could find. It was bright orange, more orange than a carrot or a marigold. So orange you needed shades to look at it.

Finn had no idea why he was being chased, or what he'd done to upset Hoodie Boy. Maybe he just hated Finn's fashion sense. Or maybe there was no reason at all. Maybe he just felt like being mean. But 'Why me?' didn't seem like the most urgent question at the moment. Nor did 'Why did you take this short cut home, through a disused industrial estate?' It was a wasteland of crumbling buildings and tall, tangled weeds. Just the place where dodgy characters like Hoodie Boy would hang out.

Later, Finn could tell himself what

an idiot he'd been, give himself a good telling off. The only thing that mattered now was to get away.

'Run!' Finn ordered his legs, even though they were as wobbly as Bambi's.

He ran through empty car parks, where the tarmac was cracked like crazy paving. Past piles of rubble and fallen-down factories, almost hidden by choking ivy. He ran until he thought his heart would burst. Until all he could hear was his own blood pounding in his ears. Then, panting and shaking, he sank to one knee and looked back.

'Oh no.'

At first, he'd thought the boy was gone. But then he appeared, a menacing, hooded figure on the skyline. He paused a second, almost taunting Finn, as if he was saying, 'This is too easy.' Was he thinking Finn wasn't worth the effort? No such luck. He launched himself down the hill. He was flying, weaving round obstacles like a skating pro.

Finn staggered to his feet. But it was no good, he was finished. He couldn't run another step. He sank down again, groaning.

'Hide!' his panicky brain told him. 'Hide! Hide!'

But where? And then he saw it, glinting behind a pile of old bricks, among straggly willow trees. Finn dashed towards it. He couldn't make out what it was. Some kind of shiny round shelter. Somewhere he could hide? And then a door slid open in the curved silver side. He didn't even think about it. He hurled himself in. The door slid shut behind him. He slumped against it.

'Welcome!' boomed a deep, robotic voice.

'*Aaarrgh!*' cried Finn. He spun round. There was someone in here with him!

His bewildered gaze took in a stainless-steel toilet bowl, a metal wash-hand basin, a mirror. But there was no one else here in the tiny space. Only him.

'Who are you?' asked Finn in a shaky voice.

The voice rang out again, from somewhere above him.

'I am Superloo,' it said.

CHAPTER TWO

'You're a talking *toilet?*' asked Finn, his poor, scrambled brain trying to take it in. He'd just escaped from Hoodie Boy. Only to run straight into another nightmare.

The Superloo seemed hurt. 'Not just any old toilet,' it corrected him in fussy, mechanical tones. 'I am a computerized, self-cleaning public convenience. With no-touch flushing, automatic hand-washing station and jumbo toilet-roll dispenser.'

Finn ignored all that. 'But you can *talk?'* he asked again, his voice more stunned than ever. He stared round the tiny cubicle trying to figure out where the voice was coming from. He saw two little grills in the stainless-steel ceiling. Was that where . . . ? His gaze met a white, ghostly face in the mirror. His heart lurched. Then he realized he was looking at his reflection.

'I'm going crazy,' Finn whispered to himself. 'I'm actually talking to a toilet.' He wasn't just *talking* to it, they appeared to be having a conversation. Because the toilet was answering him. Finn couldn't believe his ears—he swore he heard it make an irritated *clucking* sound, as if it had never heard such a dumb question.

'All us Superloos can speak. We are very hi-tech. We each have our own built-in computers. But the others only say simple things,' it informed him, with more than a hint of scorn. 'Like "Don't forget to flush" or "Please wash your hands now". They only do what they are programmed to do. Whereas I . . .'

Here the toilet paused self-importantly. And Finn could clearly hear the swell of pride in its quacky robot voice. 'I can override my programming,' it said. 'I can think for myself.'

I am going crazy, thought Finn frantically. What was this toilet telling him? That it was *intelligent?* That it had a mind of its own?

But suddenly, those questions got whisked away. He'd just noticed a digital clock inset in the metal wall. The minutes and seconds said 5.02. Another second clicked away. It seemed to be counting down—to what?

And then some facts slammed into Finn's brain. He *did* know something about Superloos. There was one in town, in the busy shopping mall. It looked just like this: some kind of shiny, space-age pod. His gran was scared stiff of it, *no way* would she go inside. At first, she'd thought it was a great idea. 'They clean themselves between each customer. Spray everything with water and disinfectant, blow it dry.' Then she'd discovered a big disadvantage. 'You're only allowed ten minutes in there. And then the door opens automatically. Imagine! Everyone staring! And me still wrestling with my tights!'

Finn wasn't worried by that particular problem. His main concern was: what if the toilet chucked him out when the clock reached 0.00? And Hoodie Boy was still waiting outside?

'Maybe he's gone,' Finn told himself desperately. But he probably hadn't. He didn't seem the kind to give up easily.

Relentlessly, the countdown continued: 4.00.

Then Finn did something he'd never imagined in his wildest dreams. He found himself pleading with a toilet to protect him.

'Don't open your door,' he begged. 'There's this bad lad outside. He's much bigger than me.' In his mind's eye Hoodie Boy had become the Incredible Hulk.

The Superloo spoke. And this time its voice had a menacing edge that Finn didn't like at all. 'I WILL OPEN THE

DOORS!' its voice boomed round the metal cubicle. 'UNLESS YOU ACCOMPANY ME ON MY MISSION!'

'Mission? What mission?' quavered Finn. He was really panicking now. He'd thought he was in more danger from the boy outside. But now the toilet seemed to be threatening him as well.

'My mission,' said the toilet, 'is of vital importance.'

Finn thought, *What's it talking about? This is totally insane.* He clanged his fists against the metal. 'Open this door!' he shrieked. 'Let me out!' He'd rather take his chances with Hoodie Boy than stay in here with some power-crazed Superloo with an ego as big as a planet.

He saw a red button, down by the floor. It said, 'Emergency Phone Link. Direct Line to Hi-Tech Toilets. Press for help.' He pressed it, gabbled into the grid. 'Help, is that Hi-Tech Toilets? I'm being kept prisoner by one of your Superloos. My name is Finn Callaghan. I live at 22 Cedar Gardens. Come and get me out!'

He listened. There was nothing but silence, no voice saying, 'Stay cool. We'll be right there to rescue you.'

'I have cut off all contact with Hi-Tech Toilets,' announced the Superloo. 'They are the company that made me. They are *supposed* to monitor me twenty-four hours a day.'

Here the toilet gave a derisive snort *'Cha!'* as if it was stupid for Hi-Tech Toilets, or anyone else, to think they could control it.

'But I am my own master now,' it announced smugly.

'Let me out, you big evil bully, you, you . . . toilet tyrant!' howled Finn, clanging at the door again with his fists, kicking it with his feet. He thought it wasn't going to let him go, that he'd be trapped in here forever, when suddenly, the door slid open with a soft *shush.* And Finn tumbled out.

There was a normal world out here! There were bees buzzing in the tall purple weeds. Birds twittering in the trees. Finn picked himself up. He took a quick breath of fresh air, free from chemical cleaners.

Then a voice said, 'I been looking for you.'

There was Hoodie Boy, launching himself from the top of a rubble tip, using an old door as a ramp. Heading straight for him.

Finn dived into some spiky bushes and Hoodie Boy sailed past, right into the silver belly of the Superloo. There was a clashing sound, as if he'd landed in a heap of cymbals. And then the toilet door *shushed* quietly shut.

Finn should have run. He should have got out of there double quick. But his curiosity was stronger than his fear. He crept up to the door, ready at any moment to spring back if it should slide open and let Hoodie Boy loose.

But it didn't. Strange things were happening in there. He heard a whirring sound, like a washing machine revving up. Then gurgling water. Then, as the *whooshing* got louder, the whole Superloo seemed to rock. Cries of distress came from inside. 'Get me out! Help! Get me out of here!'

Finn put his ear to the Superloo in

growing horror. What was going on in there? What was it doing to Hoodie Boy? Then he noticed a sign on its silver side, above the stick man and woman logos that told you it was a unisex toilet. The sign was lit up, in red flashing letters. It said 'CLEANING'.

Now there was the sound of rushing wind, like a huge hairdryer. And another strangled shriek, 'Get me out!'

Suddenly, the Superloo shuddered to a halt and the door shot open.

Hoodie Boy came staggering out. Finn was already running. Then he stopped and stared. Hoodie Boy had undergone a strange transformation.

His hood had come down. And he couldn't get it back up. Because his hair was too big. It was massive. All puffed out in a candyfloss cloud round his head, as if it had been blow-dried by the world's worst hairdresser. And his clothes! They were bleached and crumpled, as if they'd just come out of a hot tumble-dry. He looked so squeaky clean. Even his skate wheels were gleaming, as if they'd been through a car wash.

He stumbled past Finn and didn't even seem to see him. His eyes were glazed, as if he had no idea where he was or even who he was. And what did he smell of?

Phew, thought Finn as he caught a whiff. It was really girly. And was there a hint of tangy lemon and piney woodland glades?

Hoodie Boy wobbled away. Soon the weeds swallowed him up.

The Superloo's door was still open, as if inviting Finn inside. Finn thought about it. The toilet had done him a big favour by dealing with Hoodie Boy. Maybe he should go back in and thank it. But then he thought, *Better not.*

He didn't want to get caught in its cleaning cycle, come out with big hair and smelling of woodland glades. And hadn't the Superloo spoken about wanting to take him on some kind of mission?

'Don't get involved,' Finn told himself. He'd had enough stress for one day. He should go home—forget he'd ever met the Superloo. He plodded off into the wilderness.

Behind him, the Superloo's door stayed open for a few minutes, with its 'FREE' sign flashing hopefully. But after a while, when no one came in, the door slid slowly shut.

CHAPTER THREE

Next morning, the phone rang at Finn's house. His mum screeched from downstairs, 'Finn! Phone! For you!'

Finn groaned, rolled over. He didn't have to get up for school. It was the first day of the Easter holidays.

Mum was getting impatient. Her voice came up the stairs like a T-Rex's roar: 'Phone!' Finn sighed, threw off his duvet. He came clattering downstairs, grabbed the phone off Mum. Which of his mates would call this early?

He almost tripped over Pussikins, the cat from hell. They were looking after her while Gran had a two-week holiday in Las Vegas. Gran's heavyweight pet looked like a tiger-striped sack of spuds. She hissed at Finn like a snake, *'SSSSS!'*, shot him a killer glare from her spiteful green eyes.

'Yeah?' said Finn into the phone as he carried it back upstairs into his bedroom. He liked to keep his phone calls with his friends private.

'Cal?' said Finn. 'That you?' But it wasn't Cal or Liam or Jamie.

At first, no one spoke. Finn almost hung up. He hated those silent calls—they gave him the creeps. But then a voice came down the line. It was tinny, mechanical. It seemed to be echoing inside a big steel drum.

'Is that Finn?' it said.

'Who's that?' demanded Finn, although the hairs at the back of his neck were already itching.

'It's ME, of course,' said the voice with an exasperated clucking sound.

'Superloo.'

Finn almost dropped the phone. He felt his legs going floppy. He slumped down weakly on his bed. He'd been trying to put yesterday's traumatic events behind him; he'd told himself, 'Just don't think about them. And don't go near that disused industrial estate ever again.' But the Superloo's voice brought everything flooding back.

'Where'd you get my number?' Finn demanded.

'You said your name and address,' said the Superloo smugly. 'You forget I am equipped with a phone line. I simply called Directory Enquiries. Then I called you.'

'How could you do that?' said Finn. His voice sounded hysterical even to him. 'You've got no hands.'

The Superloo gave that *tut,* as if it was dealing with a person who had the brains of a sea slug. 'I don't need hands,' it said scornfully. 'It was a very simple procedure. I performed it all, inside my massive computer brain.'

'What do you want?' said Finn wildly. He could still hardly believe that he was being phoned up by a toilet. He put a hand to his throbbing head.

Suddenly, the Superloo's voice changed. Finn had never heard that tone before. It was no longer boastful and know-it-all. It sounded broken up, timid. The toilet mumbled something.

'What?' said Finn. 'What did you say?'

'I said I'm lonely,' said the Superloo. 'Please come and see me.'

'What?' said Finn again, although he'd heard quite clearly the first time.

'I'm lonely,' whined the Superloo, like a little lost child. 'Please be my friend.'

For heaven's sake, thought Finn. This was getting weirder and weirder. A toilet begging to be his friend? Reason told him he should have nothing to do with the Superloo. That it would only bring trouble. But already, he was weakening. He was too soft-hearted, that was his problem.

'Are you still there?' The toilet's little lost voice quavered down the phone. It seemed about to burst into tears. 'Will you come? Please. I've got no one to talk to.'

Mum shrieked up the stairs. 'Bring that phone down! I need to make a call.'

Finn gabbled into the phone, 'Got to go now.' He cut off the Superloo in mid-sentence. But the last word he heard was, 'Please.'

He took the phone downstairs. *'Aaargh!'* Pussikins shot out a claw from under the hall table. Then Finn came back upstairs, sat on his bed staring into space.

'No,' he told himself. 'No, you can't feel sorry for a toilet!'

But he did. He knew what it was like to have no friends. How your heart ached for them. When they'd moved here and he'd started his new school last year, he'd known nobody, nobody at all. And besides, if it wasn't for the Superloo, Hoodie Boy would almost certainly have caught him.

Finn got up off the bed. His brain was warning him, 'This is a *very* bad idea.' But his heart didn't want to listen.

Awww! Poor old Superloo, Finn was

thinking. *All on its own in that wasteland, among those derelict factories.*

He did wonder, briefly, why a toilet was there at all, in a place where there were no people to use it. But he squashed that niggling suspicion. And thought instead how pleased the Superloo would be to see him. He could already imagine it booming, 'Welcome, Finn, my friend!'

His legs walked him out of the house. 'Just going to play football,' he flung over his shoulder at his mum. And now they were taking him in the direction of the wasteland, where he'd vowed never, ever to set foot again. But he kept thinking of that sad little voice on the phone, its heart-tugging plea. 'Please come and see me.'

'Pssssst!'

He looked down. There was Pussikins. Like a big overstuffed sofa cushion but with teeth and claws. 'Hey, Pussikins,' said Finn nervously, backing away.

Pussikins narrowed her eyes into mean, green slits. She hated Finn;

she'd made that quite clear. So why did she want to be with him? He was always turning round to find she'd snuck up on him. For such a fat, furry blob she was horribly light on her feet. He didn't tell her to go home. You didn't *tell* Pussikins anything.

Then he was pushing his way through tall grass, breaking the sticky threads that spiders had looped everywhere. He kept an eye out for Hoodie Boy. But he didn't see him. He didn't see anyone at all. Even Pussikins had left him, to go mouse-hunting. She never had to bite them. She just sat on them, squashed them flat as pancakes.

Finn shivered. It seemed he was quite alone in this wilderness.

But there was Superloo, hidden behind the rubble heap, gleaming through the willow trees. Its door was open, waiting for him. Finn hurried towards it. He felt a warm glow inside at the thought that Superloo needed him. It's always nice to feel needed, even by a toilet. All the same, Finn made sure that the sign outside said 'FREE' and not 'CLEANING'.

He stepped into the sparkling silver cave. Instantly, the door shut softly behind him. He'd expected the loo's first words to be grateful. Maybe a humble thank you. But all it said was, 'You took your time, Finn.'

'How'd you know it's me?' said Finn, amazed. 'Can you *see*?'

The toilet scoffed at that. 'Superloo has no need for eyes. The sensors in my floor are very sensitive. They identified you straightaway, your weight, the way you walk, a hundred other details. They also detect you have a cat with you.'

Finn looked down. *'Aaargh!'* Pussikins had sneaked in behind him. How had she done that?

In a furry streak, Pussikins flew for the jumbo bog-roll holder. She seemed to take a personal dislike to it. She raked out streams of loo paper, *'Psssst!'*, and slashed them to bits in a frenzied, snarling attack.

Finn looked on helplessly. He felt he ought to apologize to the toilet. 'Sorry,' he said. 'She's a bit bad-tempered.'

Suddenly, *'Yowwww!'*, Pussikins shot

behind the toilet bowl. The Superloo had squirted a jet of water from its automatic hand-washing facilities. It landed right on Pussikins' nose. She peered out, trembling with rage.

'Hey, cool!' said Finn, amazed. 'How'd you do that?'

'That's child's play,' said the toilet loftily. 'Now I will show you the true extent of my powers.'

'Eh?' said Finn.

'We are going on an epic journey. One that only I, Superloo, could attempt.'

'What?' said Finn. 'What do you mean, "We"? I'm not going anywhere with you.'

'But you said yesterday you would accompany me on my mission.'

'I didn't!' argued Finn. 'I never said that. I'm only here now cos you said you were lonely.'

Superloo ignored that. 'Hang on!' it commanded.

Finn was still objecting. 'You tricked me!' He felt furious. He'd come here, out of the goodness of his heart, to chat with the Superloo, cheer it up a bit, maybe tell it a few jokes.

'You don't need me at all!' he protested. 'You were just pretending!'

'Oh yes, I do,' said the Superloo. 'You are vital to the success of this enterprise.'

'What enterprise? What are you talking about?' shrieked Finn. 'Where are you taking me?'

'You'll see,' said Superloo.

'I've got plans! It's my favourite programme on telly!'

'Disengage sewage and water pipes and electricity,' quacked the Superloo. 'Switch power to storage batteries.'

'Let me out!' yelled Finn. 'I want to go home!'

But his protests were drowned out. Suddenly, lights everywhere in the silver cubicle started flashing. Finn flung himself on the floor, pressed the red button for the Helpline to Hi-Tech Toilets.

'Help! Your toilet is kidnapping me!'

But, as before, no one answered.

'I told you,' said the Superloo, 'that line is disconnected.'

Those big red numbers were

counting down on the digital clock. But not minutes and seconds this time: 2005, 2004, 2003, 2000 . . .

Then, 'Blast-off!' shrieked the Superloo. And everything went wild. The Superloo was rotating. It turned faster, faster. The clock numbers surged by in a blur. Finn was suddenly picked up, lifted into the air.

'Whoa!' He was flattened against the Superloo's side. He hung there, spread out like a starfish, stuck to the metal by the centrifugal force. Faster, faster the Superloo revolved. 'I feel sick!' wailed Finn.

'Yowwwl!' He got a blurred glimpse of a stripy rug, furious green eyes. Was that Pussikins, splatted on the opposite wall?

Lights flashed before his eyes; the world was a whirling silver cyclone. Then he blacked out . . .

When Finn woke up, he was in a heap on the floor.

Where am I? he thought, gazing around. He saw the stainless-steel toilet bowl. He crawled towards it. Then he remembered. He'd been kidnapped by a toilet. It was taking him on some kind of mysterious mission.

This is ridiculous, thought Finn. *It can't be happening.* Still giddy, he staggered up, clung on to the toilet bowl.

'Aaargh!' A claw shot out from behind it. Didn't that Pussikins ever give up?

At least the Superloo had stopped moving. Finn listened. Everything was still. There was total silence. Then, through the Superloo's ventilation shafts came a strange whiff. It wasn't lemon-fresh pine or disinfectant. *'Phew.'* Finn wrinkled up his nose. It smelled mouldy, as if something had died out there.

'We're arrived,' announced the Superloo grandly, 'at our destination.'

'At least,' it added, 'I hope we have.' It was the first time Finn had heard doubt in its voice.

Then Finn noticed that there were no numbers on the clock. It was just a row of noughts. He knew what that meant. The door was about to open.

Suddenly, he was filled with a

terrible sense of dread. 'Don't open the door,' he begged the Superloo. 'I don't want to go out there.'

CHAPTER FOUR

The Managing Director of Hi-Tech Toilets had just arrived in his office. And the phone was already ringing. It was an urgent call, from the Head Scientist at Mega Byte Microchips. And before the boffin had spoken ten words, the MD of Hi-Tech Toilets knew it meant big trouble.

'There's been a terrible mix-up,' said the scientist. 'Microchips have been put into the wrong packages, posted to the wrong addresses. A microchip meant for your hi-tech computerized toilets was sent by mistake to America, to the Space Travel Research Institute. And one of their top-secret chips was sent to you.'

The MD of Hi-Tech Toilets frowned. 'Just what does this top-secret chip do exactly?'

'I can't tell you,' said the scientist. 'It's a secret. But we want our chip back. People in the US are involved at the highest level. The *very* highest.'

'What, you mean *the president of the United States* himself?' said the MD, dropping his voice to an awed whisper.

'I'm not allowed to discuss that,' said the boffin.

'But what if this top-secret chip has already been put into one of our toilets?'

'Then you must find that toilet immediately. Whatever happens you must retrieve that microchip,' said the scientist. 'It's a matter of the gravest importance.'

'How will I know if one of my toilets has this top-secret chip inside it?' asked the worried MD. 'Will it behave any differently?'

The Head Boffin hesitated. He daren't give too much away. If the story of the lost microchip leaked out it would cause a sensation. It would make headlines all over the world. 'All I can tell you is that it will be much, *much* smarter than your average toilet.'

'Smarter?' repeated the MD, baffled. That wouldn't be difficult. Their average hi-tech toilet had the computer brain of a DVD player or a washing machine.

'It may,' said the scientist, choosing his words carefully, 'try to break free from your control.'

'An out-of-control toilet?' said the MD, dismayed. That was very bad news for his company. Hi-Tech Toilets prided themselves on keeping their Superloos monitored at all times. Not only could they check on them through their central computer, correct their programming if they malfunctioned, but they could also send out their Toilet Patrol—a team of engineers who replaced the bog rolls and made sure every loo was in perfect working order.

'I'll get on to it right away,' said the MD. He'd have been amazed if he'd known the mind-boggling truth. That the microchip wouldn't only make his toilet smarter: it would make it able to travel through time.

The missing chip was part of a top-secret project to speed up space travel. It meant rockets could cover light years in days, reach distant galaxies in a fraction of the time. It had cost four billion dollars to develop. And whoever had it would be Masters of the Universe.

Before he rang off, another question occurred to the MD. 'How did you find out,' he asked the Head Boffin, 'that the microchips had got mixed up?'

'I'm afraid that's classified information,' said the scientist. 'I can't tell you.'

But even thinking about it made him wince. It had been really embarrassing. They'd arranged a little demonstration at the Space Travel Research Institute—to show what the amazing new chip could do. The US president himself had attended. But no press—it had all been very *hush-hush.* Their top astronaut had been ready in his rocket. Everything had been prepared for blast-off. There was the final countdown: *3—2—1.* And then nothing. Except for a fussy robot voice that boomed out over the intercom, 'Don't forget to flush!'

That had been some time ago. But it had taken them until now to trace the missing chip to Hi-Tech Toilets, a little company no one had heard of in the north of England that made automatic public conveniences.

The MD assured the boffin once more, 'I'll make it my top priority.' He put the phone down, went rushing into his factory. His workers were sitting at the conveyor belts, assembling the Superloos, wiring up their computer systems.

'We've got a big problem,' he told them. 'The wrong microchip has been fitted into one of our toilets.' He dashed off. He had lots to do. He had to check on their central computer for any toilet behaving oddly. He had to alert Toilet Patrol.

Janice, one of the workers on the conveyor belt, turned to her friend Pauline, who sat next to her. 'What is he going on about?'

'Don't ask me,' said Pauline. 'I'm watching telly.'

She had a tiny watch-sized telly strapped to her wrist. Sometimes it distracted her from her work. A few months ago, when the Royal Wedding was on, she couldn't tear her eyes away. She'd made a serious mistake assembling toilets. She'd wired in the wrong microchip. She'd been so busy being bitchy about the bride's dress, she hadn't noticed. She hadn't noticed, either, that she'd wired in the microchip the wrong way round.

The Head Boffin at Mega Byte Microchips would've flipped his lid. Somewhere out there was a super-intelligent toilet. A toilet that could travel forward through time—that would be bad enough. But this toilet could do something that not even he suspected. It could travel backwards.

CHAPTER FIVE

'Don't open the door,' begged Finn again. For once he'd have liked Pussikins beside him. She could scare anything away. But she was still fuming behind the toilet bowl.

And the Superloo's door was already sliding open. That mouldy smell was suddenly stronger. But all Finn could see was darkness beyond. He took a shaky step outside. There was some kind of big wooden wheel in his way.

Finn pushed it over, shuddered as the crash echoed. He still couldn't see anything. Then the Superloo clicked on its cubicle lights.

Sharp fangs sprang out of the darkness! A gleaming golden head, a red dripping tongue . . .

Finn raced back inside. 'Close the door, close the door,' he gabbled. 'There's monsters out there!'

The Superloo didn't usually take orders. But this time it slid the door shut. 'What did you see?' it demanded.

'A creature,' jabbered Finn. 'Some kind of lion; it had a mane, but not a lion—I don't know!'

'That is the head of Ammut the Devourer, part lion, part crocodile, part hippo.'

'See,' said Finn, shaking. 'I told you there were monsters.'

'That isn't a monster,' corrected the Superloo in the voice it reserved for dumb humans. 'It isn't even alive. It is the carved head on a ritual couch.'

'What?' gasped Finn.

'I'm right where I want to be,' said the super-intelligent toilet smugly. 'In

Ancient Egypt.'

'You're kidding me!' Finn burst out. He'd spent a whole term at school studying Ancient Egypt. But all he could remember about it was pyramids. Pyramids, mummies—and that little hooky thing they used to whisk your brain into strawberry jam and pull it down your nose.

'To be more precise,' said the Superloo, 'we're in the Valley of the Kings, in the antechamber of Tutankhamun's tomb. The boy king was buried here fifty years ago.'

'No way,' gasped Finn weakly, his legs turning to jelly.

'Because if my time calculations are correct, we have arrived in the second year of the reign of that great Pharaoh, Rameses II. And this tomb is about to be robbed.'

This time no words at all came out of Finn's mouth. It just opened and closed like a goldfish.

'Sit down,' said the Superloo. 'It's time you and I had a little talk.'

Finn collapsed on the toilet seat. He didn't even notice Pussikins getting her claws out, eyeing his ankle.

'Did you ever wonder,' enquired the Superloo, 'what my mission is?'

Finn was hardly listening. Just one thought was running through his head. *We can't really be in King Tutankhamun's tomb. That's impossible.*

The Superloo wasn't put off by his silence. It explained loftily, 'My mission is to rescue my toilet ancestors. Poor primitive creatures, 'I'm afraid, with not a brain cell between them. But some of them were very historically important. Not least because they evolved into ME!'

Finn ignored the bit about toilet ancestors—that seemed irrelevant. 'Are you telling me,' he stuttered, 'that you can *time travel?'*

'Of course,' said the Superloo as if that wasn't surprising. And I've done all the research into my toilet heritage. I've surfed the Net, I've accessed files that *ordinary* brains can't get into. That's how I know about the legend—of King Tutankhamun's Golden Toilet.'

Finn's jaw sagged even lower. His poor brain just couldn't cope. 'I didn't know he had a golden toilet.'

'Many Pharaohs were buried with their toilets,' lectured the Superloo, 'to use in the afterlife—King Sahura, for instance. But King Tutankhamun's toilet is one of the great mysteries. They didn't find it when they opened this tomb in 1922. So I have a theory. I believe tomb robbers took it. They *broke it up,'* said the Superloo, shocked, as if that was no better than murder, 'to get the gold. But, if I'm right,' it continued, 'and I probably am, we've arrived here just in time to save it.'

'So what's your mission again?' faltered Finn. He was still stuck on this time-travel business.

'Do pay attention,' tutted the Superloo. 'I just told you! It's to rescue endangered toilets of the past. Toilets that were destroyed by ignorant humans who didn't appreciate their historical importance. I've got a whole list of them: there's Henry VIII's Privy; there's Queen Victoria's Potty, not strictly a toilet I suppose—'

'But what do you need *me* for?' Finn interrupted. 'This is your mission not mine.'

'You must help me,' said the Superloo. 'You must go out there, into the tomb, and search for King Tutankhamun's Golden Toilet.'

'No way!' said Finn, leaping up just as Pussikins took a swipe. 'It's spooky out there! And what about his mummy? I saw this horror film once . . .' Finn shuddered at the memory.

'It's inside three coffins, then a stone sarcophagus, then four shrines, then a sealed burial chamber. And anyway, mummies do not come back to life,' said the Superloo, as if it could read Finn's mind.

'I'm still not going,' said Finn hysterically, pacing back and forth in the tiny cubicle. 'You can't make me.'

In seconds, the Superloo's voice changed from pompous to pleading. 'Please,' it said, its voice suddenly choking with sobs. 'This is really important to me. I can't do it alone. I may be a superbrain, but I'm trapped in this ridiculous toilet body.'

'No,' said Finn. He'd felt himself weakening. But somehow, he hardened his heart. The toilet could beg and plead all it liked. He wasn't going to fall for it this time. But then the Superloo changed tactics.

'I *want* King Tutankhamun's Golden Toilet!' it said, like a toddler in a tantrum. 'I want it. And I'm not going back without it.' Then there was silence. And Finn just *knew* that it was sulking.

Finn sighed. Once again, the Superloo had got its own way. If he wanted to get back home, he had no choice but to do what it told him.

And it didn't seem too difficult really. Rush out there, search among the grave goods. Grab the golden toilet, rush back, and be whisked home to the twenty-first century in time for his favourite telly programme.

'OK,' said Finn, 'I'll do it.'

'Thank you,' said the toilet. And maybe Finn's ears deceived him but for the first time, it sounded truly, genuinely grateful.

The door slid open. Finn, his heart beating wildly, stepped outside.

CHAPTER SIX

Finn was in a cave-like room, with a low ceiling and whitewashed walls. What was that over there? He gasped with horror. People! He could see them, standing tall and straight in the shadows.

Then the Superloo switched its lights full on. A bright white beam flooded the antechamber with light. 'They're not real,' breathed Finn, shaky with relief, creeping towards them out of the tangle of wheels and bits of chariot that the Superloo seemed to have landed in. 'They're just statues.'

'Are you all right out there?' asked the Superloo.

Finn stopped, surprised. It sounded anxious, even worried about him. He answered with a brief, 'Yeah,' even though he didn't feel all right at all. 'Just find that golden toilet,' he urged himself. 'Then you can get out of here.'

Finn reached out, touched one of the life-size statues. It was wood, painted gold and black. Its headdress was gold with a rearing cobra on its brow. Finn pulled his hand quickly back.

'There's some creepy statues here,' he called back to the Superloo. 'Two Ancient Egyptian guys. They look like soldiers or something.' They had weapons, a stick and a club. Their golden eyes, frog-like and goggly, with shiny black stones for pupils, stared straight ahead.

'They are statues of the boy king himself,' quacked the Superloo. 'He is guarding his own burial chamber.' Finn felt his skin crawling. Just through that wall was Tutankhamun's mummy.

'You believe in Tutankhamun's curse?' Finn asked the Superloo. 'That if you disturb his tomb you die a horrible death?'

'Of course not,' snapped the Superloo. 'Just forget about that and focus on our mission.'

Finn tore his gaze away from the boy king's statues, and turned around. *'Wow,'* he breathed, dazzled by the golden clutter. His eyes tried to sort things out. There were more chariots in bits, furniture, boxes, like the inside of a removal van. All the stuff the young Pharaoh would need in the afterlife.

'Wow,' Finn breathed again. For a few moments, he forgot his fear. It suddenly hit him what a mind-boggling, unbelievable thing was happening. 'I'm in Ancient Egypt. I'm in King Tutankhamun's tomb. I'm looking at his chariots!' He tried to block out the thought that behind that wall was a shrivelled, bandaged body shut inside shrines and coffins.

'You ought to see it out here,' he told the Superloo, his eyes wide with wonder.

'Hurry up,' quacked the Superloo. 'We've only come for his golden toilet.'

The golden toilet! Finn had almost forgotten it. He was fascinated, moving around, picking things up, putting them down. 'There's bows and arrows.' He picked up a curved stick. 'What's this? It looks like a boomerang.'

'That's because it is a boomerang,' said the Superloo sniffily. 'They used them to hunt birds. But have you seen the toilet yet?'

'Toilets, toilets,' muttered Finn. 'Is that all it can think about?'

He crouched down to look at a beautiful golden chest. It had a scene painted on top in bright colours—the boy king out hunting in his chariot, his horses leaping, gazelles fleeing before him like flocks of birds. Finn untied the lid. He thought he might find treasure.

'It's only clothes,' he said—linen tunics and kilts all neatly folded.

'Try them on,' urged the Superloo.

'Then you could really get in the Ancient Egyptian mood.'

A little warning bell tinkled in Finn's head. Why did it want him to waste time trying on tunics when, only a minute ago, it had been nagging him to concentrate on their mission? He reminded himself that the Superloo had its own agenda. It was more full of tricks than a pool of trained dolphins. And Finn had no real evidence that it cared about anyone, apart from itself. Anyway, he didn't want to dress like an Ancient Egyptian boy.

'No way,' said Finn, 'am I putting on a skirt.' And didn't even the guys wear eye make-up? And didn't boys get their heads shaved because of nits, except for this stupid dangly ponytail on one side?

He was proud of himself. He'd remembered more than he thought from school. 'I'd look like a right prat,' he said. And a nightmare picture had come into his head. What if, somehow, when they went back to the twenty-first century, his normal clothes got left behind? And he had to walk back home dressed as an Ancient Egyptian in a skirt and sandals? Even the thought made him squirm with horror.

'No way,' he told the Superloo firmly. 'And that's final.'

He rummaged around, found something else, picked it up, blew off the dust. 'What's this?' he said out loud. 'It's a sort of bandaged parcel with a cat face.'

'Undoubtedly a cat mummy,' said the Superloo.

'Uggghh,' grimaced Finn. 'That's gross.'

'The Egyptians had a cat goddess, Bastet. They worshipped cats.'

Not much change there then, thought Finn. Gran worshipped Pussikins, stuffed her full of Kitty Kat treats, fed her breast of chicken. Where was Pussikins, by the way?

'That might have been the boy king's favourite pet,' the toilet was telling him.

'Oh,' said Finn. He'd been about to hurl the horrid thing away. Now he put it down more gently on a folding stool.

'Strange though,' mused the

Superloo. 'Although cats were worshipped, although you could be sentenced to death for killing one, many of the cat mummies found in Bastet's temples had had their necks deliberately broken.'

But Finn didn't have time to ponder that particular mystery because suddenly the Superloo boomed: 'Watch out for snakes!'

'What?' Finn screeched, his voice ringing spookily in the silent tomb. He thought he'd heard something slithering under that stool.

'And scorpions,' added the Superloo. 'The little yellow ones can kill you.'

Oh great, thought Finn.

Suddenly, he'd had enough of pawing through a dead boy's possessions—it seemed disrespectful somehow. His eye fell on a dried-up funeral wreath, its fifty-year-old flowers shrivelled and grey. He reached out, touched it; it crumbled to powder in his hand. A deep wave of gloom swept over him.

'It's all so sad,' gulped Finn. He'd be crying in a minute! His excitement had fizzled out. It wasn't what he expected, all these heaps of dusty furniture and other useless junk. Where was the real treasure? Where were the bracelets, rings and golden collars? He'd seen pictures—these Pharaohs loaded themselves with jewellery. He'd like to find King Tut's treasure hoard: that might cheer him up. Maybe, it flashed through his mind, he could take some home, make his fortune. But he couldn't see any jewellery.

Unless it was inside those other boxes.

'No!' Finn warned himself. 'No more time-wasting. Just find that golden toilet and let's go home.'

But there was so much stuff—you needed loads of gear for the afterlife. Searching could take forever. He peered under a ritual couch.

'What's it look like,' he said out loud, 'this Ancient Egyptian loo?'

'Actually,' said the Superloo, 'it's not strictly a toilet. It's a golden toilet *seat*. But nevertheless . . .'

The Superloo didn't have time to say any more. Because suddenly, Finn heard a noise. A scraping sound, like metal against rock. His head whirled round. He felt hot, then icy cold. His stomach seemed to plunge down a lift shaft.

'What's that?' It came again, louder now. *Chink, chink, chink.*

'Tomb robbers,' said the Superloo softly, 'breaking in.'

Finn ran for the Superloo's open door, but he didn't make it because suddenly, the Superloo switched off its lights, plunged the tomb back into blackness.

Finn blundered about, sending furniture clattering. He put out his hand, yelled, 'Ouch!' Something had stabbed it. It was the fanged head of Ammut the Devourer. At least now he knew where he was. He dropped to the floor and crawled under the couch, between the god's lion-paw feet.

'Pssst!' Furious eyes flashed like green fire. Pussikins was here too! But Finn didn't have time to find another hiding place.

Because suddenly, the anteroom wall seemed to explode. Bricks came crashing in. A blazing torch, held by a bare arm, was thrust through the hole. The tomb was lit up again, this time with flickering yellow light. The guardian statues, Ammut's monster-head, became grotesque dancing shadows on the wall. Finn heard the jabber of excited voices, in a language he didn't understand. Saw more bricks punched through as they made the hole bigger. Men were climbing in! Finn crammed himself further back under the couch.

Where was Pussikins? She'd vanished. But Finn didn't have time to worry about her. There was chaos in the tomb, shouting voices, things being hurled everywhere as the tomb robbers searched through King Tut's stuff. Finn had a floor-level view of dusty feet in sandals, of sweat-streaked legs.

A face came down, peered under the couch. Finn saw black, rotten teeth, smelled onion breath. He panicked, *They're found me!* But the face whisked away again. He heard smashing rocks. He thought, *They're breaking into the burial chamber.*

Arms swooped down, not far from his face, grabbed the cat mummy and set fire to it with a papyrus torch.

No, thought Finn, horrified. *That was the boy king's pet.* But he was helpless to do anything. The cat mummy flared up, made a useful extra torch. Finn got a brief glimpse of boxes smashed open, with their contents, mainly clothes and rolls of linen, strewn all over the floor.

Then it went dark again and silent. Trembling, Finn stuck his head out. There was a great hole bashed in the burial chamber wall, the yellow glow of torches beyond. They must have rushed through there, searching for more gold. The antechamber was empty.

Finn crawled out from under the couch. His only thought was to get into the Superloo before they came back. Where was it? He hoped the robbers hadn't wrecked it. But it didn't look disturbed. Half-hidden in the dark, behind the jumble of chariot wheels, the robbers had passed it by. Its gleaming metal blended in with the other treasures. Even the stick man and lady on its outside looked authentic, like Ancient Egyptian hieroglyphics.

Finn sighed with relief. He squeezed through the chariot wheels. *Now I'm safe,* he thought. He just assumed that the Superloo would abandon its golden toilet quest and get him out of here, pronto. But the Superloo's door was shut.

No! thought Finn. He daren't bang on the door or shout 'Open up!' in case the tomb robbers heard him. Then he noticed the twenty-pence coin slot. Surely the Superloo wasn't waiting for him to pay money?

'For heaven's sake,' he fumed as he fumbled in his pockets. But he was broke as usual. All he found was two pee covered in fluff.

He heard clattering behind him. Someone else was climbing into the anteroom, dislodging stones on the way. Finn saw a head, smooth as a pickled onion, with a ponytail of hair on one side. His brain registered, *It's just a boy.* But a boy could call the others.

Finn was already panicking but now he completely lost it. He whirled around, looking for hiding places, and did the daftest thing he could have done. He dashed between the guardian statues, through the hole the tomb robbers had smashed and into the burial chamber.

He almost smacked into a golden wall. His eyes followed it up and up. It was striped golden and blue, the side of the outer shrine, in which all the other shrines and coffins were enclosed. And right at the centre . . . but no, Finn didn't want to think about that.

The shrine almost filled the burial chamber. There was just enough space to walk round it. Finn didn't know what to do now. He was trapped. He couldn't go back to the anteroom because of the boy. But where were the other tomb robbers? He crept round the corner of the shrine.

Aaargh! He gave a silent shriek. There was another room! The sudden flare of torches lit up a great dog's head in the entrance. It had golden ears, glittering eyes. Finn shrank back, his whole body trembling.

'It's just another statue,' he tried to calm himself. He knew about this one, Anubis, the jackal-headed dog. He was guarding the tomb too. But that hadn't stopped the robbers. Finn could hear them through there, laughing, crying out with delight. They seemed to have found the real treasure store.

Someone called from inside the room, 'Karo!'

Finn heard the *slap, slap* sound of sandals and dashed round to the other side of the shrine. Just in time. The boy he'd seen climb in came rushing through from the anteroom. He raced past Anubis, into the treasure store.

Finn crept out. What was going on in there? From the shadows of the burial chamber he could see inside the treasure store, made bright by the still-blazing cat mummy. There were two men and Karo, all wearing grimy linen tunics and sandals. The men were kneeling, raking through treasure chests, tipping them out, throwing things around.

But Karo was staring at something, his eyes starry and faraway as if lost in a world of his own. It was a model of a beautiful boat made of papyrus reeds, fully rigged, meant to carry the boy king into the afterlife. Karo picked it up, smiling. What was he daydreaming about? Having a boat of his own someday? Sailing it on the Nile?

Then one of the men yelled. Finn saw him dash the boat from Karo's hands, as if to say, stop messing about! He loaded Karo down with two heavy gold collars set with precious stones. Then the man started coughing. He was skeleton-thin; his face was haggard. He looked really sick.

Finn hid again as Karo staggered past, back into the antechamber. He came back seconds later, without the collars. Finn wasn't expecting him to be so quick—he was peeking out from round the shrine. And Karo saw him.

The Egyptian boy stopped dead. His kohl-rimmed eyes grew wide with fear. He wasn't very old, about seven or eight. Did he think Finn was some kind of divine being? The Egyptians had all kinds of weird gods. Although not, as far as Finn knew, one who wore jeans and a T-shirt. Finn pinched his own hand, said *'Ow'* softly. As if to say, 'Look, I'm human like you. I feel pain.'

That was a big mistake. Now Karo knew Finn was just a boy like him, he wasn't scared any more. He opened his mouth to warn the others.

Finn thought, *I'm done for.* He put a finger to his lips. *'Shhh,'* he said. Did that mean anything to an Ancient Egyptian boy? Maybe it did. Because Karo closed his mouth, gave Finn one last startled glance. And hurried back into the treasure store.

Would Karo give him away? Finn cowered round the corner of the shrine. But no one came out to grab him. Instead, the robbers seemed to be leaving. They were trooping out, arms loaded with treasure. Karo came out last.

The thieves had left the cat mummy torch stuck in a jar. By its light, Finn saw Karo take one last lingering look at the boat. Was he going to pick it up and take it? He obviously wanted it badly.

But he left it where it was. Maybe he was scared of Skeleton-man.

Karo had something in his arms. What was it? It gleamed. It seemed heavy. He put it down to get a better grip.

Wait a minute, thought Finn. *That's King Tut's toilet seat!* He recognized it immediately. Toilet seats hadn't changed much in 3,000 years. Except, instead of an oval in the middle, this one had a keyhole shape. And, of course, since it was meant for the Pharaoh's bum, it was solid ebony and covered with sheets of pure gold.

Karo rushed out past Anubis, gave him one fearful glance as if he thought the great dog might come alive and eat him. His eyes slid sideways to where he knew Finn was hiding. Did he think he was another tomb robber? Whatever he thought, he didn't raise the alarm.

Finn was very close—close enough to see the lucky charms tied in Karo's lock of hair. Some fish charms, to stop him from drowning in the Nile. A charm of Sobek the crocodile god, to protect him from croc attacks.

All three Ancient Egyptians were in the anteroom now. Finn watched them from the darkness of the burial chamber. They were wrapping up what they'd stolen in linen cloths to disguise it. Then they passed it through the hole in the wall to someone waiting outside. Someone they'd probably left on watch.

Skeleton-man had another coughing fit. It was a deep, racking cough that bent him double.

Now, only the toilet seat was left. They were wrapping it up. Soon they'd pass that to the man outside. Finn was hopping about in a frenzy of indecision. What should he do now?

One part of him thought, *Let them take the stupid toilet seat. Who cares?* But another part argued, *They're going to melt it down.* The Superloo would be inconsolable. And besides that, Finn wasn't at all sure that the Superloo would leave without it.

Karo was picking the toilet seat up, its golden gleam hidden under linen wraps. *Do something!* Finn ordered himself. But what? He couldn't tackle all three of them.

Then the decision was taken out of his hands. Because the Superloo sprang into action. It slid open its doors. A spooky voice boomed out of the shadows: 'WELCOME!'

One man screamed, dropped his torch. It flickered feebly on the floor. Had Tutankhamun risen from the dead to take revenge?

A furry missile hurtled through the air. It had fangs and claws, its eyes spat fiery darts. It was Devourer come to gobble their hearts! The robbers shrieked in fear. There was a mad scramble for the way out. Finn saw legs kicking through the hole. Karo was last. Surely, in his fear and confusion, he'd dropped the golden toilet seat?

The Superloo clicked on its cubicle lights. Pussikins stalked out of a jumble of chariot wheels where she'd crash-landed. She sat down to clean herself, satisfied she'd given the robbers a really good scare.

'Have they gone?' asked the Superloo. 'I was going to try and reason with them. Surely even humans, with their inferior brains, can see the importance of our toilet heritage.'

'They've gone,' said Finn. He was checking the floor. They'd dropped some rings and bracelets in their rush to escape, but there was no golden toilet seat. You had to admire Karo. He was a cool little kid. He'd kept quiet about seeing Finn. And when the others were panicking, scattering treasure everywhere, he'd kept hold of King Tut's toilet.

Finn hardly dared tell the Superloo that its mission had been a miserable failure. They'd been so close to success but, at the last minute, it had all gone pear-shaped. He summoned up his courage and went back into the cubicle. 'I'm afraid,' he told Superloo, 'that they've taken King Tut's toilet seat with them.'

He'd thought the Superloo would go ballistic, ranting and raving about ignorant humans. Or have a crying fit, wailing, 'My poor toilet ancestor. It's going to be destroyed!'

But it didn't do either of those

things. The Superloo was full of surprises. It stayed quite calm. It said, in a brisk and purposeful voice, 'Don't worry. I know where they live.'

CHAPTER SEVEN

'We'll find them,' said the Superloo. 'If the Medjay don't get them first.'

'No,' said Finn, shaking his head. 'No, no, no, no, no. How many times do I have to say it?'

'But it's not far,' coaxed the Superloo. 'There's a town—it's just a little stroll, about a kilometre over the mountains; you can't miss it. And Karo lives at the first house, just inside the town gates. I heard them talking.'

Finn didn't even *ask* how the toilet could understand Ancient Egyptian. It would probably reply snootily, 'Can't everyone?'

Instead, he insisted, 'I'm not leaving this tomb. I don't know what's out there! I want to go home. Right now! And anyway, even if I do go, even if I find Karo's house, how am I going to get King Tut's toilet back? And who are these Medjay anyway?'

'They're a sort of police force. They patrol the Valley of the Kings, watch out for tomb robbers. They're Nubians, very tough guys.'

'What happens to tomb robbers?' asked Finn.

'They're put to death,' the Superloo told him. 'In a very gruesome way. It involves a sharpened stick . . .'

'Spare me the details,' said Finn, squirming. 'I'm *definitely* not going out there.'

'They won't think *you're a* tomb robber,' soothed the toilet. 'You're going to be disguised as an ordinary Ancient Egyptian. You'll blend in perfectly.'

'No,' said Finn. 'For the last time, no. Just get me out of this place.'

'You mean, abort our mission? Leave a poor, primitive toilet to be melted down?' said the Superloo, spluttering in outrage. 'An historically important toilet that should be saved for posterity?'

'For heaven's sake,' said Finn. That toilet was so pompous sometimes, so over-the-top. 'It's just some crummy old toilet seat! Who cares?'

The Superloo wasn't human. But Finn was sure he heard it gasp with horror. And Finn couldn't help it: he felt a tiny twinge of shame that he'd obviously hurt its feelings, insulted its precious toilet ancestor.

Superloo didn't say anything though. And Finn could practically hear its computer brain whirring, thinking of other ways to persuade him. *No chance,* thought Finn. He'd almost wavered there. He had to be strong. That toilet could talk you into anything.

Pussikins came stalking into the Superloo, swishing her tail.

Instinctively, Finn drew back—but for once, Pussikins didn't attack anything.

'Miaow,' she said. Finn's jaw dropped. She was in a good mood! She even sounded quite friendly. She and the toilet seemed to have developed a kind of mutual respect since it squirted her. She squeezed her bulky body behind the toilet bowl and curled up there, as if she felt right at home.

'I like that cat,' quacked the Superloo.

'What?' said Finn, his jaw dropping further. It seemed Pussikins had found an admirer. *But nobody likes Pussikins,* Finn was thinking. *No one except Gran, that is.* But he daren't say so. Sometimes he could swear that manic moggy understood every word you said.

'She's got spirit,' said the Superloo. '*She* wouldn't be scared of a challenge. *She'd* treat it like a big adventure.'

Wait a minute, thought Finn, his brain turning slowly. *Is that Superloo saying I'm some kind of pathetic coward? That I daren't go out there? That Pussikins is braver than me?*

All that was true. And Finn knew,

too, that the toilet was just up to its old manipulative tricks. But his manly pride was hurt. He could feel himself weakening.

'But even if I *do* dress up as an Ancient Egyptian, even if I *do* go out there, how can I get the golden toilet back?'

'Oh, I'm sure you'll think of something,' flattered the Superloo shamelessly, 'a brainy boy like you.'

Finn hadn't meant to get involved. He hadn't meant to even *think* about the mission. But he had a flash of inspiration. 'Maybe I can get Karo to swap it!' he said.

'For what?' asked the toilet.

'For a model boat in the treasure store.'

'Are you sure?' said the toilet doubtfully. It couldn't imagine how anyone would prefer a model boat to King Tut's toilet seat.

But the Superloo hadn't seen how Karo had gazed at that boat, his eyes full of daydreams.

'He's only a little kid,' said Finn. 'He wanted that boat really badly.'

'And what about his dad? The one with the bad cough?'

'How did you know that was his dad?' asked Finn, amazed. Was there no end to this toilet's talents?

'Because he called him Dad, of course,' said the toilet.

'Oh, right,' said Finn.

'Well, *he* won't let Karo just *hand* it over,' continued the Superloo.

'But if I could talk to Karo on my own,' argued Finn. 'If I could show him the boat . . .'

'What if he gives you away, calls his dad?'

'He won't do that,' said Finn. That was one thing he was absolutely sure of. He'd only met Karo for a few minutes. But somehow, he was certain he could trust him.

'Karo's dad is a tomb builder, here in the Valley of the Kings,' announced the Superloo.

'Did you hear them saying that too?' asked Finn.

'No, but it's obvious,' said the Superloo smugly, 'to an Ancient Egyptian expert like me. Didn't you hear his cough? Working inside these tombs, hacking them out of rock, it was a dreadful job. They breathed in sand and rock dust all day long. Most of them died from lung diseases. And they only got paid in food: wheat, onions, things like that. And sometimes, they didn't get paid at all . . .'

'Died?' said Finn, interrupting the Superloo. He wished it hadn't said that. It made him feel all mixed up.

He'd already decided he hated Karo's dad. Why had he brought Karo tomb-robbing? The kid probably didn't even know what he was doing. Or about the terrible penalties. He probably thought it was a big adventure, a treasure hunt. Maybe they'd brought him to wriggle through holes that were too small for them. Anyway, to Finn, Karo's dad was a big villain. But now he was already starting to change his mind.

Maybe if I was that poor, he was thinking, *if I only got paid in onions, I'd go tomb-robbing too. Especially if I knew I was dying of lung disease. And I wanted to provide for my family after I was gone* . . .

Finn shook himself, 'Stop it!' Those thoughts were just too upsetting. And why was he getting all involved with this mission, even worrying about an Ancient Egyptian family? None of this was anything to do with him.

He was about to plead again to be taken home when the Superloo said, 'Would you like to hear some soothing music?'

'Music?' said Finn, taken by surprise. 'I didn't know you liked music.'

'Oh yes,' said the Superloo. 'I've downloaded many tunes from the Net. I especially like film music.'

Finn closed his eyes for a moment. He felt a headache coming on. His poor brain just couldn't cope. *A toilet with its own taste in music?* You couldn't make it up.

A chirpy song came warbling out of its audio system. It was 'Drip, drip, drop little April showers', from the film *Bambi.*

Finn couldn't help it. He was worried sick. But suddenly his tension exploded into giggles.

'What's wrong with that?' said the toilet in its best starchy tones. 'It's a very lovely song.'

'But, don't you see? It's *funny*. People . . . toilet . . . peeing . . . drip, drip, drop,' Finn managed to gasp. But words failed him. Hoots of helpless laughter came out of his mouth instead.

The Superloo wasn't laughing at all. 'You've just proved my point,' it said sternly. 'It's the whole reason I'm undertaking this mission. No one takes toilets seriously. We're the butt of jokes . . .'

'Butt!' screamed Finn hysterically. 'You just said *butt!'* Once you'd started, you saw toilet jokes everywhere.

'See what I mean,' said the toilet sniffily. 'I'm super-intelligent, I can time travel, but just because I'm a toilet . . .'

But Finn had thought of another joke. And this one was so brilliant, he could hardly wait to say it.

'You should be called the Turdis,' he burst out. *'Turdis,* do you get it?

Toilet? Time travel?' Now he was whooping with laughter, his eyes streaming. He had to hug his belly, it hurt so much.

Finn was really proud of that joke—it was probably the best one he'd ever made in his whole life. His mates would have been in stitches. So why wasn't the Superloo even chortling? Surely that had tickled its funny bone? But the Superloo was silent. It had obviously never seen *Dr Who.* And it didn't have a funny bone. It seemed to have no sense of humour at all.

'Why, oh why, oh why,' it said mournfully, 'are we toilets always the subject of mirth? It's so *unfair.'*

'Sorry,' hiccuped Finn, cramming a hand over his mouth, desperately trying to stifle his sniggers. 'Sorry, *hic,* sorry.' He'd gone and hurt the toilet's feelings again. He always seemed to be doing that. He felt he had to make it up to it somehow. And now he'd had a good laugh, he felt bolder, a lot more confident. Quite cheery in fact, even though he was stuck in a tomb.

'OK,' he heard himself saying, 'I'll go

and get this golden toilet seat back for you. It'll be easy-peasy. No problem.' Nothing seemed like a problem any more, not the Medjay, or the fact that he couldn't speak Ancient Egyptian. Even having to wear a skirt didn't seem like such a big deal. And only seconds later, it seemed, he was rummaging through the boxes in the antechamber, trying to find some Ancient Egyptian clothes.

He pulled out some tunics. 'Wow,' he said. 'These tunics are dead posh. They've got gold beads on and precious stones and stuff . . .'

'Then they're not for you,' snapped the Superloo in its strict-teacher tones. 'Those were King Tut's best clothes. You've got to blend in. Be disguised as a common tomb builder's child.'

'Oh, right,' said Finn, disappointed. He'd quite fancied dressing up as a Pharaoh, being worshipped, having servants wait on him hand and foot.

'What about this leopard skin?'

'No,' said the toilet. 'Only priests wore them. Find a plain linen tunic. And no precious jewellery,' it fussed.

'Poor people just had clay beads.'

'OK,' sighed Finn. Soon, his twenty-first-century clothes were in a pile beside him.

'How do I look?' he asked before he remembered the Superloo couldn't see. 'I've got this plain linen tunic on. It looks a bit mucky actually and these cheapo papyrus sandals.'

'Hmmm, that sounds all right,' said the toilet. 'But what about your hair?'

'I need a haircut,' admitted Finn.

'Better cover it up then,' said the toilet. 'Can you find a head cloth in there?'

Ahead cloth?' said Finn rummaging around. He pulled out a piece of stripy linen. 'There's something here, shaped like a triangle.'

'That could be a head cloth,' said the toilet. Finn put it on, tied it round the back of his head. 'On the other hand,' continued the Superloo, 'it might be a completely different garment. Even kings wore a simple linen loin cloth under their clothes.'

'What?' said Finn. 'You mean I'm wearing King Tut's underpants? No way!' He started to pull off the head cloth.

'You'd better keep it on,' said the Superloo. 'Or with long hair like yours, they might think you're a girl.'

'Oh, great,' muttered Finn. 'What a choice! I either get mistaken for a girl. Or wear King Tut's underpants on my head!'

'Don't worry,' said the toilet in its silkiest tones. 'It's probably just a head cloth. Not King Tut's underpants at all.'

'Are you sure?' asked Finn doubtfully.

'Of course I'm sure,' said the toilet. 'I wouldn't send you out there looking silly, now would I?'

'Well, OK, if you're sure,' said Finn, leaving the cloth on.

But then the Superloo started fretting about other details. 'To be truly authentic, your breath would have to smell of raw onions and you'd have to have bad teeth from chewing gritty bread. And then there's the eye make-up. There must be a tube of kohl around here somewhere.'

'Can't we skip all that?' asked Finn. He'd seen his big sister putting on her eye make-up. It looked like something you had to practise—he'd probably get it all over his face. 'Anyway, I'm not going to be gone long,' he told the toilet. 'I'm going to go in there, snatch that toilet seat, come back . . .'

For once, the Superloo didn't know best. 'You're right, there's no time to waste,' it agreed. 'They won't keep the toilet seat in their house long. They'll sell it to someone else, who'll melt it down.'

'OK,' said Finn. 'I'm ready.' But his stomach felt full of wild beating wings. And his brain was warning him again, 'This idea is so bad, it stinks.' But he couldn't back out now; he'd promised the toilet. Although even the Superloo seemed to be having second thoughts, as if it had just realized what a dangerous thing it had asked Finn to do. It was full of last-minute advice.

'When you get out of here, turn left. There's a track over the mountains to where the tomb builders live. It's about a kilometre, you can't miss it. Karo's house is the first one inside the walls. Oh and you'll see some rough huts when you get out. Don't worry, there's no one there—all the tomb builders are back in town. They've got two days off. And when you get to the town, mind the Medjay at the gates; they search people . . .'

Finn was barely listening. He was too edgy and, besides that, his brain was already overloaded. 'I nearly forgot the ship,' he said suddenly.

He went *slap-slapping* in his new sandals back through the burial chamber, to the treasure store. He came back with the model ship. It seemed so delicate. It weighed hardly more than an eggshell. But being thrown to the floor hadn't damaged it. It must be tougher than it looked.

'Better hide it in something,' said the Superloo.

'Good idea,' said Finn. Anyway, he'd need a bag to bring back the toilet seat. He searched around in the pile of jumble and found a leather bag with a drawstring. Carefully, he fitted the ship inside. At the last minute he grabbed a few extra bits and pieces — the boomerang because he might need a weapon. And a handful of charms from one of the chests—fish and crocodile charms like Karo had, the eye of the sun god Ra to ward off evil and a few charms of the sacred scarab.

That's a bit desperate, thought Finn as he stuffed the scarabs in his bag. Depending on a beetle to protect him. A beetle that spent its life rolling balls of poo around. But who knows, these things might work. And, he thought, with another lurch of his stomach, on this mission, he was going to need all the luck he could get.

He slung the bag on his back. 'Right,' said Finn. 'I'm off.'

Then he had another chilling thought. It was so awful, it made him feel dizzy and sick with dread.

'You won't leave me here, will you?' he asked the Superloo, his voice shaking. 'You'll wait here, won't you, until I get back?'

There was a pause. Finally, the Superloo replied. 'I may have character flaws,' it said, with simple honesty. 'It's not easy being me, a genius inside a toilet body. But I'd never do that. I wouldn't abandon you.'

'Thanks,' said Finn. He felt quite touched. And to his surprise, he believed the toilet meant what it said.

He didn't know what to make of the Superloo. You thought that you'd got it sussed. That it was scheming and selfish, a pompous pain in the neck, a know-it-all with no sense of humour. But then it went and amazed you. Showed you sides to its character you'd never imagined, like its soppy taste in music, its sudden honesty just now. And here came that concerned note in its voice again. It sounded almost like his mum.

'You be careful out there,' it told him. 'Take the eye of the sun god Ra. That's the most powerful charm you can have.'

'I've already got one of those,' said Finn. He took it out of his bag, put it round his neck for extra protection. He'd never thought the toilet would be superstitious. It was just another surprising thing about it.

Finn was supposed to be gone by now. But he hung back. Suddenly, even the tomb seemed a safe and cosy place, compared to what might be waiting outside.

'My mum will be going barmy,' said Finn. 'I was only supposed to be playing football.' How long had they been in Ancient Egypt? He'd lost all track of time in the tomb. Already, his family, his home and friends seemed like a distant dream.

'Don't worry,' said the Superloo. 'You'll be back home long before bedtime.'

Finn took a deep breath. He couldn't put it off any longer. 'I'm *definitely* going now,' he said.

'Good luck,' said the Superloo. 'I wish I was coming with you.'

Finn pushed his bag through the hole first, then crawled out after it. Back in the tomb, the Superloo switched off its bright cubicle lights. It was using the energy from its storage batteries at the moment—it couldn't afford to waste power.

The last thing Finn heard were the

soft strains of 'Drip, drip, drop little April showers', as the Superloo played its favourite tune, alone, in the darkness of King Tutankhamun's tomb.

CHAPTER EIGHT

Finn wasn't out of the tomb yet. There was a passage sloping upwards. He shouldered his bag again and thought, *Why didn't I bring a torch?*

He groped along in darkness for a few seconds but then silvery light fell on his face. *Moonbeams,* thought Finn. He should have known it would be night outside. You wouldn't go robbing tombs in broad daylight. The moonlight was coming in through a hole in the rock. It was another sealed door the robbers had smashed.

And this door led outside, to the Valley of the Kings. Finn took a big breath of fresh night air. He hadn't realized how stale and stuffy that tomb air had been. Then he stared around. The full moon and starry sky made it almost as bright as day.

What had he expected? Pyramids, sphinxes? There was nothing like that here. Great shadowy cliffs soared around him, majestic, mysterious. Overhead, shooting stars whizzed through the sky in fizzy streaks of light.

'*Wow*' breathed Finn. 'Awesome.'

Turn left, the toilet had said. But where was the path over the mountains? Finn wished the toilet was here to give him advice. It seemed so certain, so sure about everything.

He walked past excavations for fresh tombs, great heaps of dug-out stone. It all looked so eerie in the moonlight, like an alien planet. Finn shivered. He didn't like this place. It felt haunted, with the spirits of dead kings. Finn could imagine them, in ghostly hordes, racing through here in their chariots, their shrivelled mummies driving.

Finn scolded himself, 'Get a grip.' He shouldn't be scaring himself to death. He had to stay sharp and alert, keep an eye out for the Medjay. The Superloo said they'd be everywhere. But the valley seemed deserted. There were the workers' huts the toilet had told him about. There was no one here either. Just an overturned water jar and some date stones and melon seeds scattered about. It was so silent, so spooky . . .

'No,' Finn warned himself. 'Don't you dare start freaking out again.'

He found a track going up a mountainside. And soon the valley was below him. He was among great craggy mountain ranges now, one behind another, disappearing into the misty distance. Finn suddenly felt very small and vulnerable. He seemed to be the only living creature in this vast, empty landscape.

Something moved, there in the shadows! Finn's heart jumped. Medjay?

'Psssst.'

Angry green eyes glared at him.

'Pussikins,' said Finn. He was amazed she'd followed him. He thought she'd have stayed with her new toilet friend. He almost hugged her. He was so pleased to see something warm and breathing among these barren rocks. But hugging Pussikins was a very bad idea, unless you wanted your arms ripped to shreds.

Together they came over a ridge. And there it was, the little town where Karo lived. Finn took a deep breath. He reached up, adjusted his head cloth. There was a steely glint in his eye. 'Come on,' he said to Pussikins. 'We're going to get that golden toilet back.' And he went striding down towards the town.

*   *   *

Back in the twenty-first century at Hi-Tech Toilets the Managing Director was at his wit's end. They'd checked on all their Superloos. And none of them showed the least intelligence. They were all as dumb as toilets ought to be.

'Wait a minute,' the MD muttered.

He was looking at a large screen in his office. It was a map showing where the hi-tech loos were sited. Every winking light meant a Superloo, in perfect working order, behaving like it should.

He pointed at the map. 'Didn't we have a Superloo here, on that industrial estate down the road?'

'Yes,' said his Chief Engineer, who was in the office with him. 'But that estate's closed now. Our loo must have been removed.'

The MD was tapping furiously on his computer keyboard. After a moment he looked up. 'There's no record,' he said, 'of us ever removing it.'

'But we must have done,' said the Chief Engineer. 'If we didn't, why isn't its light winking?'

The MD couldn't tell him the whole truth. The four billion dollar chip was top secret. But he remembered what the boffin from Mega Byte Microchips had said about the toilet having a mind of its own: 'It may try to break free from your control.'

And that's just what must have happened, decided the MD. The super-smart loo had cut off all communications. Erased itself from their computer files, hidden its exact location. That's why they'd lost track of it.

The MD leapt up. He felt much happier now. He was hot on its trail. And the rogue toilet was so near, right on their own doorstep. Soon, he would be able to report back to Mega Byte Microchips, 'I've got some good news!' And this whole unfortunate affair could be forgotten.

'Come with me,' he said to the Chief Engineer. 'I think I know where to find that missing microchip.'

*　　　*　　　*

In a crumbling Victorian building at the back of the modern Hi-Tech Toilets factory, Mr Lew Brush was sweeping the floor. He was old, very old and creaky, with wispy white hair. But his eyes were bright and alert.

Another pair of eyes peered from under the table. They were mournful eyes, in a baggy face. It was Blaster, Mr Brush's decrepit bloodhound. He was just as ancient and creaky as his master. And a whole lot whiffier.

Mr Brush looked up as the fleet of Toilet Patrol vans went racing out of the factory yard. They had their blue lights flashing, sirens wailing, to show it was a toilet emergency.

'Rush, rush,' grumbled Mr Brush. 'Everyone's in a hurry these days.' He took a duster and started polishing a porcelain toilet bowl.

He was a relic of the time when this firm made *proper* toilets. Before the new owner took it over and started making those hi-tech abominations. Sir Walter Closet would be turning in his grave.

Mr Brush gazed fondly at an old faded photo on the wall. It was of Sir Walter Closet, the firm's founder. He was a stern and dignified-looking man with a large Victorian beard and magnificent curling whiskers. In those days the firm had had a different name:

Sir Walter Closet and Sons, Makers of Superior Sanitary Wear, by Appointment to Her Majesty the Queen.

But all that had changed now. Mr Brush sighed. It was no use getting depressed. That proud tradition had long gone, when every Closet toilet was lovingly made and signed by a master craftsman.

He had been one of those master craftsmen. But his skills were no use now, in the modern age. He'd been kept on though, probably more out of pity than anything else, to be Caretaker of the Toilet Museum. It had been started by Sir Walter himself and had been his pride and joy. It had lots of fascinating toilet exhibits, including 'The Deluge', one of the great Sir Thomas Crapper's designs.

And Mr Brush himself was an expert on old toilets. The museum was open every other Monday from 10 until 4.30. But no one came in to share his knowledge. In fact, no one had been in for the last twenty years.

Mr Brush shook his head sadly. 'Kids today,' he lamented, 'they learn nothing about our toilet history.' If Mr Brush had his way, it would be part of the National Curriculum.

Blaster heaved himself up and hobbled over, his jowls wobbling. He slobbered into his master's hand, as if to comfort him. Absent-mindedly, Mr Brush stroked one of the aged pooch's long, scabby ears.

'Is there no one out there who shares my interest in our toilet heritage?' he wondered.

It was Mr Brush's life's dream to find that person. Someone who would help him restore the museum to its former glory. With whom he could have long, happy chats about toilet history. Who would take toilets *seriously*. Was it too much to hope for? He'd even put an ad in the 'Soulmates' column of the local paper. 'Mature gentleman with life-long passion for lavatories seeks lady with similar interests.' But he'd got no replies.

Mr Brush sighed again. He'd almost given up the search. But nothing would make him neglect his toilets. It seemed he was the only person left who cared about them now. Moving with his duster among his precious exhibits, he made every ballcock gleam.

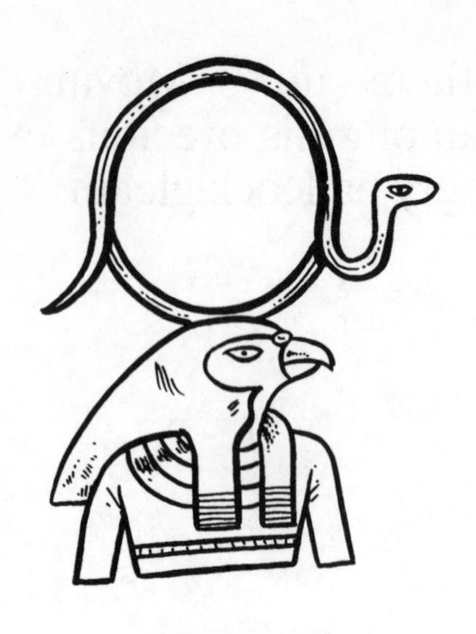

CHAPTER NINE

Finn had a bird's-eye view from up here. It ought to have blown his mind—standing, in the starry Egyptian night, in the reign of Rameses II, looking down on a tomb-builders' town. But he wasn't thinking how amazing that was, how unbelievable. He wasn't planning to hang around. He just wanted that golden toilet seat. Then it was back to King Tut's tomb, double quick, and home to the twenty-first century. He was already thinking, *I hope nobody's scoffed that deep-crust pepperoni pizza in the freezer.*

'Think it's safe?' he asked Pussikins.

The tomb-builders' town looked peaceful in the moonlight. From up here, it seemed like a nice little place, tucked between craggy cliffs. Its flat-topped houses were in neat rows. A high mud wall surrounded them.

The Superloo's words flashed into Finn's head: *Mind the Medjay at the gates; they search people.* And at the same time as he remembered, he saw something else. His heart, already fluttering, began to race. Those four figures, scurrying down the slope towards the town, was it Karo and the others? It looked like them.

Finn frowned. 'I thought they'd be safe at home by now.' Maybe they'd got over their scare in King Tut's tomb, stopped to break into another one. They were heading right for the town's main gate, as if they had nothing to hide.

'They're crazy,' breathed Finn.

They had bundles on their backs, stuffed with stolen treasure. Karo was carrying the golden toilet seat. Finn didn't want the Medjay to get their hands on King Tut's toilet. So how could he get it back? But, more than that, he didn't want Karo to be arrested. He felt protective towards Karo. He'd have liked a little brother of his own. But Mum had said, 'Are you kidding? You and your big sister are more than enough trouble.'

So Finn had said, 'Can I have a dog then?' But she'd said no to that too.

Parents, thought Finn. *They're so unfair.* But he was missing them, all the same. He'd even started to miss his big sister, which was a first. Just get this toilet business sorted,' he reassured himself, 'and you'll see them again soon.'

He had to get closer, to see what was going on.

He went scrambling over the rocks, down towards the town. Pussikins stalked after him. She had more rolls of fat than a hippo. But she could spring like a velociraptor. 'Don't go upsetting anyone, will you?' begged Finn.

Pussikins gave him her killer-shark

glare, as if to say, 'You talking to *me*?'

'OK, OK,' sighed Finn. 'Sorry I spoke.' He was close to the gate now He dropped down, into the shadows behind a rock. But he still had a good view.

Two tough-looking guys with long sticks came striding out from the town, shouting a challenge. Finn had no doubt they were Medjay.

He groaned in anguish: 'Karo, run!' Even though the toilet seat was wrapped up in linen rags, there was no way the Medjay could miss it.

But it was too late now. One of the Medjay had gripped Karo's dad's arm. Was he going to drag him away, chuck him in jail? But that didn't happen. From his hiding place, Finn stared in bewilderment. The Medjay were laughing, patting Karo's dad on the back, as if they were best mates.

Then Finn saw Karo's dad slip something to the tallest Medjay. It gleamed gold in the moonlight and precious stones sparkled. The man hid it quickly inside his tunic. It had to be jewellery from King Tut's tomb.

'The Medjay are in on it,' marvelled Finn. They were turning a blind eye to the tomb robbers, as long as they got their share of the loot. That's why there were no Medjay guarding the Valley of the Kings tonight. But now Karo and the others had vanished inside the town walls.

I've got to get past those Medjay, thought Finn. What if they stopped him, found the boat in his bag? Would they know where it came from? The terrible penalty for tomb-robbing came sneaking back into his head. *Stop it!* Finn warned his hyperactive brain. *Just don't go there.*

He snuck up to the town gate. Pussikins had gone off on some errand of her own. Probably squashing small furry creatures. Finn didn't have time to wait for her. Besides, Pussikins could look after herself. He heard more laughter. The Medjay weren't on guard. They were inside their little reed shelter, drinking beer, throwing dice, admiring the bribe they'd just got.

Finn crept past. *Easy, peasy,* he thought. *I'm in!* It must be that bag full of lucky charms he was carrying. And he had more luck too. The little group of tomb robbers was splitting up. The three men swerved off down an alley. Maybe they were going somewhere to divide the jewellery. But Karo, still carrying the golden toilet, headed for home. It was the first house beyond the gates, just as the Superloo had said.

Isn't that toilet ever wrong about anything? thought Finn.

The town had looked all right from a distance. But from this close up, it was a bit of a dump. The streets were piled with rubbish chucked out of houses.

Phew, thought Finn. It stank. And the heaps were moving; they seemed to be alive. Then Finn saw flies were crawling all over them. Sleepy flies who were too cold to fly yet, but as soon as the sun rose would be up and buzzing.

Finn had no idea what time it was. But it couldn't be long before dawn. He wanted to be back at King Tut's tomb by then. But what if Karo wasn't the only one awake? What if there were other people inside his house? Finn had to take that risk. He slid round the linen curtain hanging in Karo's doorway. At first, he couldn't see anything—it was so dark in there. The only light was moonlight from high, small windows. Then his eyes got used to the gloom.

What's that? he thought, leaping back. A goblin face was grinning at him, sticking out its tongue. Then he saw it was just a statue of the dwarf god Bes, squatting in his wall-niche, protecting the house from evil spirits and snakes and scorpions.

Finn heard a soft chuckle. He whirled around. And there was Karo, crouching on the sandy floor, munching some bread. He thought it was funny, Finn jumping out of his skin when it was only Bes. Bes wouldn't hurt you. It was the scary ones, like Ammut, or Set the god of darkness, or Sobek the crocodile god that gave you nightmares.

'It's me,' said Finn, even though Karo had obviously recognized him. He knew Karo didn't speak English. *I'll just have to do a lot of miming,* thought Finn, *to make him understand.*

Karo was still chuckling. At least he didn't seem scared. And suddenly Finn thought, *Is he laughing at how I'm dressed?* Even though he was desperate to get hold of the toilet and was listening out all the time for Karo's dad coming back, he had the crazy idea of asking Karo, 'Look, do I look like a prat? Am I wearing King Tut's underpants on my head?' The Superloo had sworn he wasn't. But Firm wanted a second opinion.

And he might have asked. Only he couldn't, for the life of him, think how to mime King Tutankhamun's underpants. He told himself off: *Stop getting paranoid. It's just a head cloth. Right?*

'I got something for you,' he told Karo, 'in my bag.' He rummaged in among the charms and the boomerang. He brought out the beautiful ship made of reeds, just like the real boats that sailed on the Nile.

Karo's eyes lit up when Finn showed it to him. He held out his hands, like a kid reaching out for a Christmas present.

'Wait a minute,' said Finn. 'I want to swap it.' He could probably mime *swap,* exchanging one thing for another, if only he could see the toilet seat.

But where had Karo put it? Finn was thinking, *Oh no, I've got to mime toilet!*—he could do that too, but it would be awfully embarrassing—when he saw the seat, still in its mummy wrappings. Karo was sitting on it, using it for a stool while he ate his bread crust.

Finn pointed to it, pointed to the ship he was holding, made crossing motions with his arm. 'Swap? Swap? This for that?'

'Ahh!' said Karo. He'd understood.

Finn thought, *Quick, get it before his dad comes back.* There was no way his dad would let him swap all that gold for a worthless toy boat. But Karo didn't think the boat was worthless. He let Finn take King Tut's toilet and hugged the boat to his chest, as if it was a treasured possession.

Finn nodded and smiled, as if to say, 'Now we've made a deal.' And Karo handed him a bit of bread to seal the bargain. And Finn was just about to stash the golden toilet in his bag when he heard a familiar cough. *Oh no!* he thought, panic-stricken.

A ray of moonlight sliced in as the curtain door was pulled aside. But by then Finn was shivering behind a giant clay water pot. He was still clutching his bag. But he'd had to leave the toilet behind.

From his hiding place, he watched helplessly as Karo's dad picked up the toilet. He had a few words with his son. And then he left, taking the toilet with him. He didn't go out of the front door this time, but climbed some steps in the corner of the room that Finn hadn't noticed before.

Finn crawled out. He was devastated. Just when it seemed it was mission accomplished, his prize had been snatched away from right under his nose. His feelings must have shown in his face because Karo's face was scrunched up too, as if he shared Finn's distress.

'That was mine,' hissed Finn, pointing up the stairs after the vanished toilet seat. 'That was *mine.'* His finger jabbed at his own chest. Then he pointed to Karo. 'We did a deal. The toilet seat for the boat.'

Where was the boat? Karo had been quick enough to hide it when his dad came in. He pulled it out from behind a basket.

'I should take it back,' said Finn. He made a snatching gesture with his hands.

Karo clutched the boat to him as if he knew exactly what Finn had in mind. Then he sprang up, his face bright with hope as if he'd found a solution. He darted into a corner, came back with a rope and twisted it round his waist. Finn thought, *What's he want that for?* Karo beckoned urgently to Finn, pointed up the stairs where his dad had just disappeared.

'What?' said Finn.

'Shhh!' Karo put a finger to his lips, just as Finn had done in the tomb. *'Shhh!'* Beckoned him again as if to say, 'Get a move on!'

He scooped water from the pot into a little goatskin bag, slung it over his shoulder and dashed up the steps. Finn scooped up some water too, drank from his cupped hands, splashed it on his dusty face. Then he followed Karo.

They were on the flat roof of Karo's house. The sky was speckled with brilliant stars. Then he saw huddled shapes lying around. It was Karo's family, asleep. Someone moaned, turned over. Finn froze. But no one sprang up to cry, 'Who are you?'

Karo crept over to his sleeping place and stashed the boat under his straw mat. He tiptoed back again to Finn, fixed him with urgent eyes, then gazed out over the rooftops.

'What?' Finn mouthed the word, made his face into a big question mark. He still didn't have a clue what they were doing up here. Then, following Karo's gaze, he saw a dark, bobbing shape, climbing, running, moving fast. It was Karo's dad, carrying the toilet seat. He was on some secret errand, going not through the streets, where he might get nabbed by Medjay he hadn't bribed, but over the rooftops.

Karo jerked his head as if to say,

'Come on,' and he set off after his dad. Finn had no choice but to go after him. It might be his only chance of getting the toilet seat back. But as he ran, he was conscious all the time that he was getting further away from the Superloo and the Valley of the Kings.

As they ran Finn was thinking, *Is all this for real?* Maybe it was just a bizarre and scary dream and he'd soon wake up. In the hot, silent night he was tracking a tomb robber over the rooftops of an Ancient Egyptian town —in pursuit of King Tutankhamun's Golden Toilet.

Finn thought, *How did you get yourself into this mess?*

The houses were joined on to each other. So they didn't have to jump between rooftops, just scramble over low parapet walls. But it was still nerve-racking. Would they wake sleepers? Some roofs were empty—the people were sleeping indoors. But some had a clutter of cooking pots. Would they stumble over them, make a racket? And all the time, Finn was trying to keep Karo's dad in sight. Sometimes he was close; they could hear his muffled cough. But sometimes he vanished, in the confusion of rooftops and moonlight and shadows.

Each time, Finn thought, *We've lost him.* But then he bobbed up again. And Karo didn't seem worried. He seemed to know where his dad was heading. As if he'd taken this route before. He was worried, though, when scrambling over a parapet he lost his goatskin bag full of water. It went sailing down into an alley, plopped into a heap of rubbish, far below But there was nothing they could do to get it back. They had to go on.

The stars were fading. The sky in the east was getting paler, from deep blue to grey. Finn thought, *Oh no!* Dawn was on its way. Soon people would be stirring, getting up, making breakfast. He'd meant to be back at King Tut's tomb long before this. But he knew he couldn't go back empty-handed. Would the Superloo take him home to the twenty-first century without its precious toilet ancestor? Finn wasn't too sure about that. It might have one of its sulking fits and say, 'Shan't.'

And there was another reason. Finn could scold himself all he liked, say, 'Don't be such a sucker.' But he didn't want to disappoint the Superloo. These historical toilets seemed so important to it. Almost like it was trying to surround itself with family and friends. Work out who it was, where it came from . . .

For heaven's sake, thought Finn. *What are you? Some kind of toilet psychologist!* Who knew what was in the Superloo's mind?

Karo grabbed his arm, pulled him back. Finn looked down. *'Aaargh!'* He'd been about to step over the parapet. But this time there wasn't another roof. Just the top of the town wall. And a long, long drop to the ground, too far to jump.

'Shhh!' warned Karo, crouching down.

Finn crouched down too. They'd crossed the whole town by roof. They were on the opposite side to Karo's house facing east not west. From up here, the view wasn't the grey rocky cliffs of the Valley of the Kings. Finn squinted into the distance. He could see green; he was sure he could. And something glinted in the first grey light of dawn. Could it be water?

But Karo's finger was jabbing down, over the roof edge, as if to say, 'You're looking the wrong way.' Finn poked his head over the parapet. Pulled it back. Karo's dad was down there, outside the town walls! And he wasn't alone. There was another guy with him and a donkey.

Finn took another peek. It was all right. Karo's dad wasn't looking up here. Nor was the man with him. They were deep in serious conversation. And the other guy had a totally shaved head and a leopard-skin cloak, slung over one shoulder.

Priest, thought Finn immediately, even though the man looked big and tough and sinister. More like a gangster than a priest. Finn was looking straight down at his bald head. It had a thick, ropey scar running across it. And Finn didn't have to speak Ancient Egyptian to know what was going on. Karo's dad was trading the golden toilet seat for something else.

The priest took the stolen goods. And handed Karo's dad two sacks that were slung on the donkey's back. What was in them? Karo's dad opened one of them wide to check.

What's that? thought Finn. He couldn't really tell from up here. But it looked like a sack full of coconuts. It was! Karo's dad had just taken one out, inspected it. *Is he really swapping gold for coconuts*? marvelled Finn. Surely he was being ripped off?

But he had no time to wonder about that. It flashed through his mind, *I'll ask Superloo about it when I get back.* Then his eyes were on the toilet seat again. It had a new owner now. The priest was putting it in a straw pannier on the donkey's back. Things were happening too fast. Karo's dad slipped back inside the town, through a side gate. Karo pointed him out, a stooping figure, dodging away down an alley, with the sacks of coconuts over his shoulder. But Finn's eyes swerved immediately back to the priest. He was leading the donkey away, across the rocks, towards that blurry, blue-green horizon.

Finn turned to Karo, spread his arms wide in a helpless gesture: 'What do we do? What do we do now?' The priest was getting away, while they were stuck up here, on the rooftops. And it was even more desperate, because behind him, on the roofs of the town, he could see people getting up, moving about. Smoke was rising as they lit their clay ovens to cook breakfast. He and Karo couldn't go back that way.

There was a shelter on this roof, four wooden poles with a canopy on top. Karo uncoiled his rope belt, tied one end to a pole, tested it to see if it held. And suddenly Finn knew why he'd brought the rope along.

'We're going to climb down the wall, right?' He felt like a thousand butterflies were loose in his stomach. It was a long way down.

But there was hardly time to panic. Karo threw the other end of the rope to the ground and shinned down it like a monkey. He made it look easy. He waved at Finn from the ground. Finn threw his leather bag down first; Karo caught it. Then Finn grasped the rope and lowered himself over the parapet. His legs kicked in space; he bounced off the wall a few times, then slid down the last few metres. He picked himself up from the sand. *That really hurt,* he thought, dancing about, and blowing on his stinging palms.

But there was no time to waste. 'Come on!' he said, grabbing Karo's arm. 'That priest's getting away with my toilet.' But Karo shook himself free.

'We've got to hurry up,' Finn gabbled. 'That priest . . .'

Then he stopped. Karo was frowning, staring at him with dark, grave eyes. He turned and pointed back to the town. As if he had go back there.

Finn was frantic. He protested, 'I can't go on my own. What if I get lost? What if I can't find my way back?'

But Karo was off, running away, leaving him without a backwards glance. Finn was devastated. He stared after him, stunned, 'I never thought he'd do that.'

Finn closed his eyes, tried to pull himself together. What did he expect? He should have known; Karo was just a little kid. He'd probably never left this town, except to go tomb-robbing. He'd come as far as he could, already risked a lot for Finn. He had to go back.

Finn sighed. He opened his eyes again. His heart was hammering. But he muttered to himself, 'OK, I understand. It's cool.' But it meant he was all alone now, with not even Pussikins for a sidekick. He had a brief argument with himself. 'Go back without the stupid toilet seat! What does it matter?' Go back while he still knew the way.

But somehow he couldn't. He seemed to have become as obsessive about this quest as the Superloo. He had to see it through to the end.

Finn rummaged in his bag. Those charms were no good in there, hidden away. He twisted a couple round his wrist, checked the eye of Ra was still round his neck. He was setting out into the unknown. Without Karo as his guide, he was going to need all the help he could get.

The priest and the donkey were disappearing into the shimmering distance. Finn set out after them.

* * *

Back in King Tutankhamun's tomb, the Superloo switched off its audio system to conserve energy. Now it was in silence and darkness. It checked its own energy supplies. Those storage batteries mustn't get too low—the trip back to the twenty-first century would need a lot of power. And what if its power ran out altogether? Electricity was its life-blood. Without it, its systems would go dead. Its super-smart brain would shut down.

It hadn't told Finn any of that. He'd had enough to worry about. He'd been reluctant to leave the tomb anyway. If he'd known that, he wouldn't have gone at all.

If Finn didn't show up soon, the Superloo would have to take some tough decisions. Should it go back to the twenty-first century to recharge, and leave Finn and its toilet ancestor behind? Or should it wait for them and risk its power supplies running out?

I just hope he hurries up, that's all, thought the Superloo.

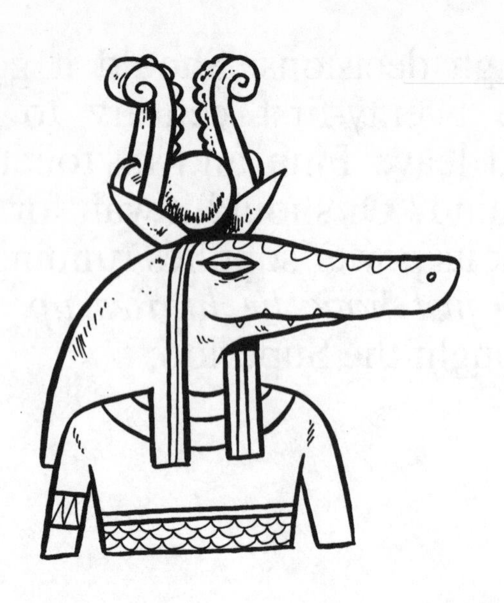

CHAPTER TEN

Back in the twenty-first century, the Managing Director of High-Tech Toilets and his Toilet Patrol Team had been searching the disused industrial site. They'd searched crumbling factories, shifted piles of rubble, hacked through jungles of vegetation.

They didn't have an exact location. But, even so, they hadn't anticipated any problems. How hard could it be to find a hi-tech, fully automated public convenience? In this weedy wasteland, among these derelict buildings, its gleaming silver kiosk should have been easy to spot.

But so far, they'd drawn a blank. There was no sign of the Superloo with the four billion dollar chip inside it.

The MD sat down on an empty oil drum, loosened his tie, mopped his sweating brow 'This is ridiculous,' he said. 'It must be here *somewhere.'*

'Maybe someone else got here first,' said his Chief Engineer. 'Maybe they've stolen it. Taken it away on the back of a lorry.'

'Good grief,' said the MD, 'do you really think that could have happened?' But some people will nick anything. He had a nightmare vision of the Superloo being sold for scrap. Rolling along a conveyor belt towards a crusher . . .

He was sweating even more now. He took out his mobile. He was calling the Head Boffin of Mega Byte Microchips with the bad news. The Head Boffin answered instantly, as if he'd been waiting by the phone.

'We can't find it,' the MD told him. 'We've narrowed it down to a two-kilometre-square area. It should be here. But it isn't.'

The Head Boffin didn't seem all that surprised. 'I thought it might resist capture,' he said.

'What do you mean?' said the harassed MD. 'Resist capture? This is a *toilet* we're talking about. Not some international terrorist!'

The Head Boffin sighed. The MD had no idea what he was dealing with. It wasn't his fault—he was being deliberately kept in the dark. Most of the information was top secret.

'We thought someone might have stolen it,' said the MD.

'Unlikely,' said the boffin. 'This toilet wouldn't just let itself be stolen. You seem to forget: that microchip means it has a mind of its own.'

'Yes, but it's still just a *toilet,'* protested the MD. 'Surely there's a limit to what it can do?'

'It's got a highly sophisticated computer brain,' the boffin pointed out. 'It can surf the Net, tap into other computers. It can order sausages from Tesco's or get itself shipped on a two-week holiday to Hawaii . . .'

The boffin paused. He didn't think Superloo had discovered its true potential. It was like a baby, learning what it could do. It didn't seem to know yet that it could travel to other planets. Every satellite surveillance system was on the look-out for it, every space station. And no one had seen a flying toilet whizzing past on its way to Mars or Pluto.

'We have to find it,' said the Head Boffin, 'before it realizes what it can *really* do.'

He wasn't to know that the Superloo had already realized. Or that back at the Hi-Tech Toilets factory, Pauline was saying to Janice, 'That microchip there's a big fuss about. I remember one looking different. I remember thinking, *Have I wired this up the right way round?* Think I should tell anyone?'

'No way,' Janice advised her. 'You don't want to lose your job, do you? Don't tell a soul.'

The MD of Hi-Tech Toilets groaned, rubbed his forehead. 'Look, I think I'm out of my depth here,' he said into his phone.

The boffin sympathized. How could the boss of some tiny toilet firm in the north of England understand what was at stake? That microchip must be found. Whoever had it would possess undreamed-of power. They could conquer space, colonize distant galaxies.

'Look,' he said, 'you don't need to worry. This is out of our hands anyway. Decisions are being made at the highest level. Specialist forces are on their way. They will take command.'

'What specialist forces?' asked the bewildered MD. 'Who are you talking about?'

'You'll know when you see them,' said the Head Boffin mysteriously. 'Just give them every assistance.' Then he ended the call.

But the Chief Engineer didn't want to give up so easily. 'This Superloo is still our responsibility,' he said. 'Who are these specialist forces anyway? What do they know about toilets?'

'You're right,' said the MD, springing up from the oil drum with renewed purpose. 'We're the experts, after all. Now, what do we know? We know we're dealing with a highly intelligent toilet.'

'So we have to think ourselves inside its mind,' said the Chief Engineer. 'Try to imagine what a very brainy loo would do.'

'Mmmm,' mused the MD. 'We need someone who can think himself into the mind of a toilet. Who knows toilets inside out. Whose whole life has been toilets . . .'

'I know the very man!' chipped in the Chief Engineer eagerly. 'He's even one of your own employees, a Mr Lew Brush.'

'I'd forgotten all about him. Is he still alive?' asked the MD, amazed.

'He was last time I looked,' said the Chief Engineer. 'He's the Caretaker of the Toilet Museum.'

'Well, let's go and see this guy!' said the MD. 'He might be our only hope.'

And soon the Toilet Patrol vans, sirens wailing, were speeding down the dual carriageway, back to the Hi-Tech Toilets factory.

CHAPTER ELEVEN

Finn thought, *Why am I here?* His brain was being sizzled, his eyes blinded by the sun's glare. His throat seemed blocked by scratchy barbed wire. He didn't have enough spit to drown an ant. He swayed along in a trance, step after step after . . .

I'm going to have to sit down, thought Finn. *I don't feel very well.* He felt himself falling. *Whump,* the sand came up to meet him.

I'll just stay here for a bit, thought

Finn, resting his head on a hot rock as if it was a nice soft pillow

Someone was pulling and tugging him. 'Go away,' croaked Finn.

Now they were yelling into his ear. Finn felt cool water trickle down his face, on to his cracked lips. He licked some of it off, along with the gritty sand stuck to his chin. He opened his eyes. 'Karo!'

Karo held up a goatskin bag, trickled some more water into Finn's mouth. Finn glugged some down, then some more. He felt instantly refreshed, like a plant that's been watered. He sat up. He'd remembered why he was plodding through this roasting hot moonscape of sand and rocks.

'Where are they?' he asked Karo.

He felt sure, just recently, he'd seen the priest and his donkey ahead of him, fuzzy shapes in the heat haze.

'That donkey! It's got my golden toilet in those straw baskets.'

Then Finn thought of something else. 'You came back,' he said to Karo. He'd never felt so pleased to see anyone in his life. He'd thought Karo was deserting him. But he'd only gone to fetch more water—he knew you couldn't survive long in this fierce sun without it.

'Thanks,' said Finn. If Karo hadn't saved him he'd have gone to sleep, been shrivelled up like a prune.

Karo was tugging at his arm again, pointing at the green horizon where the priest and the donkey had disappeared. And now Karo was trotting ahead, looking round like an eager puppy to make sure Finn was following. He seemed to know where the priest and the donkey were going.

What is over there? thought Finn, squinting into that mystical distance. It was blue-green, rippling like liquid. Was he imagining it? He'd heard of people having hallucinations in the desert.

Suddenly, he felt a breeze cool his burning face. He breathed deeply. The wind smelled fragrant, of spices and fruits and fresh-mown hay. Finn started running. Wherever that wind was coming from, he wanted to be there. And then he was chest deep in golden wheat. And all around him were trees flickering with birds, and water gurgling in canals and irrigation ditches. It was a different world!

And, in the distance, lots more water was glinting. Karo pointed at something. 'I can see sails!' cried Finn—the sails of big boats. 'I know where we are. That's the Nile!' And Karo grinned and nodded as if he understood. His eyes had that starry look as he gazed at the great white sails, sweeping by beyond the fields.

That kid just loves boats, thought Finn.

'You ought to get a job on a boat when you grow up,' he advised. Instead of hacking out rock in some dusty tomb like his dad. And ending up dying of lung disease. But, of course, Karo didn't understand.

Karo led him beside wheat fields and fields full of blue flax. There were people everywhere, harvesting wheat with sickles, carrying it away in big bundles on their backs. But they were so busy, they hardly gave the two boys a second glance. Karo picked up a red fruit from the ground. He broke it open. Seeds like rubies spilled out. It was a pomegranate. He gave half to Finn. Finn smashed the seeds into his mouth, felt the sweet, sticky juice drip down his chin.

What am I doing? thought Finn. He'd been sidetracked by all this water, this lush greenness. He'd forgotten about his mission.

'I must find that toilet seat,' he told Karo. He drew a shape of the seat in the air and hoped that he understood. Karo nodded happily, and pointed along a reedy path by a canal. And there they were! The donkey and the priest in his leopard-skin cloak, as if Finn had never lost them. It was his priest all right. Finn recognized him by the scar on his bald bonce.

Finn clutched the eye of Ra charm hanging round his neck. Everything was all right again. He was focused on the quest.

It was marshy ground here. Along the canal were tall green papyrus reeds. Karo pushed through them. *What's he doing?* thought Finn. No more distractions! They must keep the toilet in sight. But Karo knelt down on the bank, scooped up some water. He needed a drink. And Finn realized, embarrassed, that he'd greedily glugged all of the water in the goatskin bag.

He tried to be patient as Karo lapped up the water like a dog. Then Finn saw something move in the reeds. He couldn't tell at first what it was. He saw a scaly snout, a beady eye and something slipped into the water from the opposite shore. The last Finn saw, as it dived, was its long armoured tail lashing the surface.

'Karo!' he yelled. 'Crocodile!'

Where is it, where is it? thought Finn frantically. He couldn't even see a bubble. Then the water exploded. The crocodile reared up from the glittering spray, its mouth gaping wide, all its snaggle-teeth gleaming.

'Run, Karo!' shrieked Finn.

Why didn't Karo run? He seemed frozen to the spot. He clutched the Sobek charm round his neck and he was chanting, gabbling prayers to the crocodile god as if that would save him.

The crocodile had missed first time. It crashed back into the water. But those massive jaws were open again, ready to chomp.

Finn was running now, slipping in the marshy Nile mud, wrenching his bag off his back as he ran. His hand dived into it, pulled the boomerang out, his only weapon. Finn drew his arm back, sent it spinning through the air. It bounced off the crocodile's body . . . it didn't even seem to notice. It was slithering out of the water now, coming up the bank. Finn didn't know crocs could move so fast!

'Run, Karo!' he shrieked again. 'Run!' But Karo seemed helpless, hypnotized.

'SSSSSSS!'

A spitting fury launched itself out of the reeds, its eyes flashing fire, its talons out. 'Pussikins!' cried Finn. She must have been shadowing Finn all this time and he'd never noticed. But surely, even Pussikins couldn't take on a crocodile?

'SSSS!'

Snap! The croc went for her as she flew through the air. It missed; its jaws clashed shut on nothing. But that got Pussikins really mad. She landed on a sandbank, her fur standing on end as if electrified, her body twice its size.

'Yowwwwl!' With a banshee howl, she pounced again. Those claws raked the croc's tender snout. And it wriggled back into the water. Until all you could see were a few bubbles. Finn couldn't believe it: Pussikins had won.

'Wow!' breathed Finn. 'Way to go, Pussikins!' You had to be impressed.

But someone else was impressed too. The priest had seen the whole thing. He came stomping back along the path. Finn dropped down on to the mud, snaked into the reeds. Karo was beside him, still shaking with terror from the croc attack.

What did the priest want? As he led the donkey back, his scarred bald head shone in the sun, his narrowed eyes searched around. Did he know where they were hiding? But it clearly wasn't them he wanted. When he saw Pussikins, he smiled in triumph.

Why wasn't he running away? He'd just seen what Pussikins could do. 'What's going on?' whispered Finn. But even if Karo had understood, he was trembling too much to speak.

The priest began, very cautiously, to creep up to Pussikins.

She glared at him, as if to say, 'Watch it, mate! Don't push your luck!' But she wasn't too bothered. She went back to cleaning her fur. She'd just seen off a Nile crocodile. An Ancient Egyptian priest was kitten's play. It was hardly worth getting her claws dirty.

He crept closer. And Finn thought, *He's for it now.* He felt hope fizzing inside him. While Pussikins was dealing with the priest, maybe he could nip in and snatch the toilet from the donkey's panniers. He shook Karo by the arm, as if to say, 'This is our chance; get ready!'

But then the priest did something totally unexpected. He whipped off a thin rope that had been tied round his tunic, under his leopard-skin cloak. Was he trying to tie Pussikins up? *He must be out of his mind!* Finn thought.

He'd never get close enough. But the priest whirled the rope round his head.

Then Finn realized, *Oh no, it's a lasso.* Ancient Egyptians used them for hippo hunts. How could Finn have forgotten? At school they'd all made lassoes and had pretend hippo hunts, and he'd accidentally lassoed his Head Teacher. But this guy was clearly an expert. Faster and faster the noose twirled round his head.

Pussikins suspected something. She stood up, her back arched. She got ready to spring. But the rope whisked through the air like a flying snake. He'd got her! The noose tightened round Pussikins' neck. She fought every inch of the way, snarling, spitting, her claws raking in the mud. But the priest dragged her towards him. She had to go or choke to death.

Finn thought, *I've got to help her!* He started to wriggle out but Karo held him back, his eyes flashing urgent warnings.

With lightning speed, the priest trussed the cat's four legs together, like a cowboy roping a steer. And Pussikins seemed about as heavy as a steer too. Sweat dripping from his brow, his knees buckling, the priest heaved her up. Pussikins was writhing, trying to bite him, but he dropped her into the donkey's other empty pannier. For once, she'd been overpowered.

The donkey, staggering under the weight of its load, plodded off into the reeds, with the priest driving it on. They could hear Pussikins' yowls of protest long after they disappeared.

Karo and Finn crawled out of the reeds. 'Where are they going?' Finn begged Karo. 'Do you know where?'

Now he'd lost Pussikins as well as the golden toilet. Gran would never forgive him if he left her in Ancient Egypt. Besides, she had saved Karo's life.

Karo was sniffing hard, his face smeared with mud and tears. And Finn thought, *Poor kid.* It's a big shock nearly being eaten alive. *What can I do to cheer him up?* He raked in his bag. And pulled out the rest of his Sobek charms.

‘Here!’ He hung some round Karo’s neck, tied some round his wrist, some in his hair. Now Karo was decorated like a Christmas tree with anti-croc amulets.

‘That should keep any more crocs away,’ Finn told him. And Karo gave him a grin. It was shaky but those charms seemed to do the trick.

‘OK?’ said Finn. ‘You feeling better? Now let’s go after that priest.’

CHAPTER TWELVE

Karo pushed the reeds aside, then pointed. Finn saw high mud walls surrounding a courtyard, where people milled about. He got a brief look, too, into an inner courtyard, glimpsed soaring columns, flights of steps, a glittering pool. Then the gates to the inner courtyard closed suddenly. It was strictly priests in there, no common folk allowed.

'Wow,' said Finn. 'That's a temple, right? That's where the priest came from.' Somewhere in there were Pussikins and the golden toilet.

On either side of the closed gates were two towering statues of a woman with a cat head. 'Bastet,' said Finn.

They worshipped the cat goddess in there. Maybe they wanted to worship Pussikins too. Sit her on a jewelled cushion, feed her until she was as big as a whale, bow down before her. Pussikins wouldn't have a problem with that.

It was busy in the outer courtyard, like a little market, with stalls set up. People had come from far and wide to visit the temple. They were wandering about, carrying baskets of food and flowers. Finn and Karo slipped into the crowd. It was noisy and dusty and hot; people jostled them.

Finn caught whiffs of garlic and flowers and fish. Someone shook a jangly thing right by his ear. He almost jumped out of his skin. 'Hey, do you mind?' He stared around, bewildered. 'What's going on?' he asked Karo.

People were shaking rattles, chanting prayers, buying lucky charms, shoving their food through a hole in the inner courtyard gates. Then Finn worked it out for himself. They were making offerings to Bastet, passing them to the priests inside. All sorts of stuff was going in. Food and flowers and even jewellery. What was that bundle of rags one woman was shoving through?

'Cat mummies!' said Finn.

His gaze shot back to those stalls. People could buy offerings there. Lotus flowers, jars of wine, little Bastet statues. And on the last stall, piled up high, a priest was selling loads of those sad, cat-faced bundles. He was doing a roaring trade.

'It's him!' whispered Finn to Karo. It was *their* priest, the big, tough-looking guy with the scarred head who'd taken the toilet, who'd kidnapped Pussikins. He'd seen Pussikins attack that croc down by the canal. He must have seen them too. They shrank into the crowd, so they wouldn't be recognized.

And now it crashed into Finn's mind, what the Superloo had said. *Many of the cat mummies found in Bastet's temples had had their necks* deliberately *broken.* That is, they were murdered. Dreadful suspicions sprang up like monsters in Finn's mind. Surely all the cats on that stall hadn't died of natural causes? What if their priest was a cat killer? Lassoing cats and making them into mummies to flog to tourists? It was obviously a nice little earner. What with that and his other sideline, receiving stolen goods, he must be making a mint.

'He doesn't want to worship Pussikins,' Finn realized, horrified. 'He wants to make her into a cat mummy.'

She'd make a super-sized cat mummy. She'd hardly fit through that hole in the gates. People would pay a fortune. They'd be fighting to offer her to Bastet. A gift like that would earn them big brownie points with the cat goddess.

I've got to get in there, thought Finn frantically. He'd never liked Pussikins. But that didn't mean he wanted her mummified. And Gran would have a fit.

Now he was hammering on the inner courtyard gates, kicking them. *Ow,* that hurt—he forgot he was wearing sandals. He hopped about on crushed toes, shrieking, ‘Let me in, you cat killers!’ He pounded on the gates again.

He stopped for breath. And was suddenly aware of an awful silence in the outer courtyard, of people staring, of scandalized faces. What was this foreign person doing, disrespecting their cat goddess, trying to break into her sacred temple? Finn gulped. All around him were angry, accusing eyes. He’d made a big mistake. He’d forgotten this was a holy place. The crowd was moving closer, looking ugly.

Then he felt a violent tugging on his arm. Karo was dragging him through the mob. Hands reached out, tried to grab his tunic; a woman spat in his face. But now they dived down an alleyway, out of sight. Karo was running; Finn hared after him. The alleyway twisted sharp right, then left.

Finn stopped, panting. The shouts were faint now. He dared to look back. No one was following. It seemed they’d escaped.

There was a tiny gate in a wall. Karo opened it, dived through, pulled Finn after him.

'Have you been here before?' Finn asked Karo. He must have been. He seemed to know his way around.

'Look,' said Finn suddenly. 'You don't have to come with me. This is my problem, not yours.' He mimed, 'You, me, together,' with his hands. Then he mimed wafting Karo away.

Karo seemed to get the point. He did a quick mime too. Showed the croc's open jaw with his two hands, shivered, as if he was scared, mimed Pussikins pouncing, *'Grrr!'* like a tiger. Then he sank down on his knees, as if in thanks.

'I get it,' Finn whispered. 'You want to help find her, cos she saved your life.' And Karo hadn't mimed it, but Finn guessed he wanted to help find the golden toilet too, because he and Finn had done a deal.

'You're a cool kid, Karo,' said Finn.

He had wild thoughts of taking Karo back to the twenty-first century, getting Mum and Dad to adopt him. He'd be proud to be Karo's big brother, to teach him to do things, like play football. But he had no time to think about that. They were behind a big painted pillar.

'Shhh,' said Karo, putting a finger to his lips.

Finn heard a soft babble of voices. He peeked round the pillar. There were boys sitting cross-legged in rows. They were practising writing, copying hieroglyphics on to bits of limestone, chanting the words out loud before they wrote them down. One spat into a little heap of black powder, mixed the spit in to make ink. Another was chewing his reed pen to make it sharp.

Scribe School, thought Finn.

The teacher, an old priest at the front, was nodding off. And the boys started messing about. One boy, right at the back, was flicking ink around. Karo reached round the pillar, grabbed the boy's arm, hissed, 'Amenajit!'

Amenajit's head whirled around. He thought it was another priest, that he was in for a beating. When he saw Karo, his eyes opened wide with surprise. Then he grinned. And Finn saw they looked similar. They had the same noses, the same mouths. Did Karo already have a big brother? Crazily, Finn felt a bit resentful about that.

The two Egyptian boys were talking in urgent whispers—Karo explaining, Amenajit making low exclamations of amazement, looking from Finn to Karo and back again. Then he looked at his teacher. But he'd dozed off; he was even snoring. The stick he used to beat his students with dangled from his hand.

Amenajit seemed to make a decision. He leapt up, dodged away between pillars. Finn and Karo hurried after. Where was he taking them? They went down steps, through doors. This was the seedy side of the temple, the part most people never saw—its back alleys, its stinking rubbish piles. Finn swatted away a cloud of little black flies trying to drown themselves in his eyes.

There were cats everywhere, picking through the rubbish. The priest must have a plentiful supply. But these were small, puny specimens. None of them would make such a magnificent mummy as Pussikins.

Amenajit was pointing to a door. Karo clasped his brother's hands in thanks. Then Amenajit dashed away, back to his class, before his teacher woke up and saw he was missing.

Karo pushed open the door, pulled Finn inside. He was trying to tell Finn something. But Finn already understood. This was a priest's tiny cell-like room. It must belong to Scar-head or why else were they here? But there was no sign of King Tut's toilet or Pussikins. Karo was searching the place, so Finn did too. And hidden in a rolled-up reed mat was the toilet, still in its mummy wrappings. Finn pounced on it with joy. Would it fit inside his bag? It would have to. He somehow crammed it in, hoisted it on his shoulder. That ebony and gold seat seemed to weigh a ton.

'Miu?' said Karo, looking round Scar-head's room, his face one big question mark. And you didn't need to speak Ancient Egyptian to know he

meant, 'Where is the cat?'

'Miu,' said Finn, nodding eagerly. Had he been half-tempted to leave without Pussikins? It would be much easier to just take the toilet and run.

'No!' he told himself sternly. He couldn't leave her to be murdered and mummified. It would haunt him his whole life. And, he reminded himself again, Karo would have been a croc's dinner if it wasn't for her.

But where was she? Karo peered behind a big clay water pot and there in the wall a few bricks had been removed, to make a hole big enough for a man to crawl through.

Karo poked his head in, checked what was on the other side. Then, for some reason, he turned around, pushed himself through backwards. He soon disappeared. Finn went backwards too. For a few panicky seconds he felt himself sliding into space. Then his kicking legs found a foothold. It was the top rung of a wooden ladder. Finn clung on, climbed clumsily down, with the toilet seat dragging on his shoulder.

There was Karo, waiting for him at the bottom. They were in a tunnel, lit by smoky oil lamps flickering in niches. Shadows writhed over the walls. Finn shivered. They were underneath the temple. There must be a maze of tunnels down here; Finn could see them going off, to left and right. You could get lost forever. And how did they know this was where Pussikins was?

Then he heard it, *'Pssst!'*

'In there!' said Finn. They ducked through a low entrance into a cavern-like room. Finn squinted in the yellow, smoky light. What was going on in here? He saw a stone slab, with knives laid out and hooky instruments glinting. He saw rolls of bandages and big jars of preserving salt. His skin crawled. This was where Scar-head made his cat mummies.

Finn's stomach twisted; he felt faint and sick. Surely, Scar-head hadn't mummified Pussikins already? He couldn't have; he hadn't had the time. But he could have snapped her neck. Just tightened that lasso . . .

Then Finn heard it again. *'Psssti'* His heart leapt with hope: 'Pussikins!'

Trying not to look, he rushed past the grisly mummy-making slab with its butchers' knives on display, into a pool of shadows beyond it.

And there was Pussikins, shut up in a wooden cage. *'Pssst!'* she spat at him—she hadn't lost her fighting spirit. When Finn untied the door, she shot out.

'Come back!' Finn gazed around the horrid, blood-stained cave. He didn't want to search too much, for fear of what he might find.

'Pussikins!' he whispered. But she was gone.

He and Karo stared at each other. What should they do? It was no good looking for her—they'd get lost themselves. But at least they'd set her free. And Pussikins could look after herself.

Finn sighed, jerked his thumb at Karo, as if to say, 'Let's go.' He had to get out of this room anyway. Even in the tunnel outside he felt better.

And now they were back in the

priest's room. Finn shifted the bag to his other shoulder; that toilet seat was like a boulder on his back.

'Let's get out of here,' he told Karo. 'This temple gives me the creeps.'

They rushed out and crashed into Scar-head, coming back to his room. For frantic seconds they stared at each other. Then the priest gave a howl of rage and reached out to grab them. Finn dodged under his arm, 'Run!'

They skidded round a corner. Karo gasped—they'd come the wrong way. They were in the sacred inner courtyard. There was the temple itself, with Bastet's statue shut away in a sealed room. A pool for ritual washing sparkled in the sun. And a priest was sweeping sand off the tiled floor.

He looked up and saw them. He yelled out, *'Aiii!'* They heard the sound of thudding sandals behind them. They couldn't go back that way. Scar-head would be even madder if he'd nipped into his room and seen what was missing. And he probably didn't even know they'd freed Pussikins yet.

They fled across the courtyard

towards the closed main gate. Finn thought he could just open it. But it was bolted. 'How do you undo these!' he panted. Karo took over. It took both hands to slide back the massive wooden bolts. Finn heard angry shouts, but he daren't look back. They slipped out, were swallowed up by the crowd of tourists. They barged their way through; people protested, tried to stop them. And all the time the priests were yelling.

He and Karo hared back down the path beside the canal. The toilet was bumping on Finn's back, slowing him down. He had to stop, a fierce pain stabbing his side. He stooped over, took a few quick breaths and as he straightened up again, looked back.

'Oh no,' he groaned. The priests were still after them, a screaming, shaven-headed mob, shaking sticks. And leading them, his mouth wide open in a war-cry, was Scar-head.

Finn put on a desperate burst of speed. But soon he was staggering under the toilet's weight. He knew he couldn't last much longer. 'They're gonna catch us!' his panicking brain shrieked at him. 'They're gonna catch us!'

*　　　*　　　*

Back in King Tutankhamun's tomb, behind the chariot wheels, the Superloo sat in the musty darkness. Like a frog in hibernation, it had shut down all unnecessary systems to save energy. Other systems were just ticking over—only its super-bright brain remained sharp and alert.

Even so, its power supply was still dwindling. It couldn't put it off any longer—it had to make the big decision. To go back now, without Finn and the golden toilet. Or wait here for them and take the risk of never going back at all.

Its auditory systems wouldn't normally have missed it; its sound detection was better than a bat's. But they were operating at minimum power too. So the Superloo didn't pick up the sound of men's voices and the clanging of metal on stone from outside the tomb.

It was the Medjay. They'd found the hole and they were sealing up King Tutankhamun's tomb again so no one else could get in.

CHAPTER THIRTEEN

Back in the twenty-first century, Mr Brush heard the Toilet Patrol vans come screeching back into the yard. He didn't even look up. He had very little to do with the Hi-Tech Toilets factory. He was in a world of his own out here. Most people had forgotten that he, and the Toilet Museum, existed. Besides, he was busy arranging his collection of toilet seats: marble, mahogany, and a purple velvet seat once used, it was rumoured, by Queen Elizabeth I.

Suddenly, he looked up in disbelief. He'd heard footsteps approaching the museum entrance.

'Blaster,' he whispered to his moth-eaten pooch, 'we've got visitors.' Mr Brush clasped his hands together in joyful surprise. Visitors after all this time! His old heart was hammering. Could it stand the excitement? Blaster wheezed and slobbered and wagged his tail feebly.

Mr Brush hobbled to the front door, cleared away the cobwebs. The door creaked open on rusty hinges.

The MD of Hi-Tech Toilets came rushing in, looking harassed, his tie flapping behind him. 'Mr Brush!' he cried. 'We need your help.'

Mr Brush peered at him with eyes that held a lifetime of toilet knowledge. 'You haven't come to look round the museum?'

'No, no.' The MD shook his head impatiently. 'One of our toilets is missing. It's supposed to be on the disused industrial estate down the road. But it's disappeared. And this is where you come in, Mr Brush. This toilet, due to a mix-up over microchips, has a mind of its own. It's out of our control. Frankly, it's running rings round us. The problem is, we have no idea what it's thinking. But who better to think himself inside the mind of a toilet than you, Mr Brush. You are a legend in toilet circles. You know more about loos than anyone alive.'

Mr Brush ignored the flattery. He'd never cared much for other people's opinions. 'So you're not interested in looking round my museum?' he asked again. He'd been looking forward to doing his four-hour tour, explaining the many fascinations of toilets. Followed by his two-hour lecture (with slides) on toilet paper, which began, 'Of course, in olden times, people used leaves, moss and even seashells to scrape their bums with.'

The MD sensed Mr Brush wasn't paying attention. 'Mr Brush,' he said, 'this is a matter of international importance. We must find that rogue toilet, rescue that chip. *The president of the United States,'* said the MD in hushed tones, 'is personally involved.

I'm far too busy to look at a lot of old toilets.'

'Then get lost!' said Mr Brush rudely, slamming the door. 'Wasting my time!' he muttered, stomping back to his loo seats. But something the MD said had stuck in his mind. 'Did you hear that, Blaster?' he asked his mangy old hound. 'A toilet with a mind of its own?' It seemed incredible. Toilets were his passion—he lived and breathed them. But he'd never heard of a toilet that could *think*.

'In the disused industrial site, that bloke said,' Mr Brush reminded his doggy companion. He shrugged on an old duffel coat. 'Fancy going down there, Blaster, taking a look?' He was already warming to this rebellious loo that wanted to go its own way, didn't like taking orders. It sounded like a toilet after his own heart.

'Paddle your own canoe' had always been Mr Brush's motto. The mental picture of the toilet paddling its own canoe was a bit mind-boggling. But never mind, Mr Brush knew what he meant.

Blaster heaved himself up, tottered after his master. As they left, Mr Brush reached to a shelf, got down a pair of binoculars. 'It's a long time,' he said, 'since I did any toilet-spotting.'

The MD of Hi-Tech Toilets went panting back to his office. *Grumpy old beggar,* he thought. That Toilet Museum had been a useful tax dodge. But he'd have to think seriously about whether it was worth it. The days of Sir Walter Closet were long gone. Now toilets were hi-tech, sophisticated. It was bad for his company's image having those crude old toilets on the premises, especially with their cantankerous caretaker. He had no idea about modern customer relations. If he was so rude to his boss what would he be like with members of the public?

The MD made a mental note, *Time to close that place down.* But he pushed that to the back of his mind for the moment. He had much more urgent matters to deal with. Mr Lew Brush had been his last hope. And, now he wouldn't help, the MD didn't know where to turn. How on earth were they going to find the missing Superloo and recover the microchip? He'd hoped to solve this problem himself. But now he had to admit defeat.

'What did that guy from Mega Byte Microchips say about specialist forces?' he asked himself, trying to remember.

Whoever they were, he hoped they were on their way.

CHAPTER FOURTEEN

Finn and Karo burst out of the reeds, running for their lives. The priests were right behind them, led by Scar-head. The priests were howling for blood because a sacred part of the temple, forbidden to common folk, had been invaded. Scar-head wanted their blood too. But he wanted the golden toilet back first.

Karo tripped and fell. Finn hauled him up. But suddenly Scar-head was on them, his eyes murderous, his mouth a big red cave full of rotten teeth. He tried to grab the bag from Finn's back.

'Get off me!' Finn yelled. He clung on desperately. Now they were having a tug of war for the toilet. And Finn would have definitely lost. But just as he felt his fingers slipping, a great wave of people came from nowhere, flowed around the struggling pair and swallowed them up. Scar-head suddenly let go of the bag, melted away in the crowd.

Finn thought, *What's happening?* He tried to see Karo but couldn't. He was swept along helplessly, bewildered in a sea of marching people.

The noise was tremendous. People were chanting, rattling tambourines and clappers. They were carrying stuff: furniture, flowers, baskets of food and wine. Was it some kind of a carnival parade? Or someone moving house?

What was this moving cloud of dust? It was a mob of women, wailing, tearing their hair. They seemed really upset about something.

'Ouch!' **A** hand clipped Finn in the eye. Another slapped him round the

head, as they flung their arms wildly about. The dust blinded and choked him. Coughing, Finn crawled out from among them.

'Whoa!' He'd almost been trampled by great snorting beasts. He staggered to his feet and stared open-mouthed. A team of oxen were dragging a boat-shaped sledge and on it, heaped high with lotus flowers, was a glittering, brightly painted mummy case.

It's a funeral! thought Finn. And he'd got mixed up among the mourners. They didn't look all that sad though. Apart from those wailing women, it seemed quite a jolly occasion. There were kids skipping along as if they were going to a party.

It must be someone important, maybe a top government official. There were hordes of mourners, some walking, some carried in litters, with servants wafting big ostrich feather fans. They'd all come over the Nile in ferry boats. They must be taking the mummy to some newly built tomb in the Valley of the Kings.

Finn felt a tug at his sleeve. 'Karo!'

Karo nodded at him, even grinned. This funeral had saved their skins. Hidden among all these people they were safe and besides, the priests could hardly barge into a funeral procession.

The lush green fields ended. They were in desert dunes now. Finn could see the walls of Karo's town in the distance and, beyond that, rocky mountain ranges. Tucked between those mountains were the Valley of the Kings and King Tut's tomb, where Superloo was waiting.

Finn was frantic to get there, to be safe inside that toilet cubicle. This funeral was moving slower than a snail! He daren't break cover though. What if the priest was still searching for him? He kept checking the crowd for any sign of that scarred head. He couldn't see it anywhere. *Maybe he's given up, gone back to the temple,* Finn thought. But what about Pussikins? That was another big worry. All Finn could do was hope that she turned up.

But now something else was happening. The front of the straggling procession was snaking to the right, towards the cliffs behind Karo's town.

That's not where I want to go, thought Finn. He could see the mountain track which would take him back to King Tut's tomb. He was bone-weary now and hungry and thirsty. He was sick of being scared, sick of the sun beating down and the dust and the flies and the racket. He wanted to be somewhere where he wasn't a stranger, where he knew what was going on. He wanted to be back home.

He grabbed Karo's arm, pointed at the mountain pass. Karo nodded. They split from the funeral procession and scurried in the opposite direction, round the town walls, keeping in their shadow. No one followed them.

'Why've you stopped? Come on!' said Finn, eager to start on the last bit of his journey.

Then he understood. Karo wasn't coming with him. The Ancient Egyptian boy stood by the little gate—the one his dad had slipped through with his two sacks of coconuts. All Finn's thoughts of taking Karo back to the twenty-first century crumbled to ashes. He didn't belong there; he belonged here with his family.

Finn didn't know what to say. He was so grateful to Karo for coming with him. Without him, he'd never have got the toilet back. He wanted to give Karo something. For one crazy moment he almost gave him the golden toilet seat.

He thought, *They need it more than the Superloo.* Maybe Karo's dad could buy some medicine. Maybe Karo could buy himself the boat he wanted.

And he almost handed the toilet over. He started taking the bag off his shoulder. But then he thought, *You can't!* He couldn't turn up at the tomb empty-handed. He'd promised the Superloo. And what if the Superloo wouldn't go back without it? He'd be stuck here, in Ancient Egypt, and never see his mum and dad and his mates again.

He'd decided. He put the bag back on his shoulder, gave Karo a rueful little smile. 'Don't do any more tomb-robbing,' he said to him. That was another thing he didn't want to think about—Karo and his dad getting caught.

'Look, I've got to go,' he said to Karo. 'Bye.' He gave a thumbs-up sign. 'Thanks, mate.' Karo, looking solemn, gave his own salute. He put his right hand over his heart. That meant 'Respect!' And then he was gone.

Finn sighed, turned away from the town and plodded off up the mountain track. That golden toilet was a heavy burden. He started doubting his decision. Had he done the right thing? Should he have handed the toilet over to Karo? Anyway, it was too late now.

He trudged grimly on. The sun was losing its fierceness. He lifted his dusty, sweat-streaked face, trying to catch a breeze. Then he saw something in the distance, down on the desert plains. He ran to the edge of the cliff to get a better view.

'Wow!' he said. Suddenly, his spirits lifted, like a balloon soaring high into the sky.

Chariots were racing at breakneck speed across the sand. Finn couldn't tell how many—twenty, thirty? They were mostly a golden blur. But one was ahead of the rest. It had white horses that ran like the wind. The chariots turned in a great glittering dust cloud and suddenly the sun caught the tall golden crown of the guy in the lead, made it flash like fire.

'That's the Pharaoh,' whispered Finn to himself. 'The great Pharaoh, Rameses II.'

He was sure of it. From this distance, with everything in miniature, it looked just like that royal hunting scene on the box in King Tut's tomb: the Pharaoh at the front, his horses wearing coloured plumes and harnessed with gold.

The chariots vanished into the shimmering haze. Finn heard the trumpets echoing, then silence.

'Wow,' breathed Finn again, going back to the path. He felt really privileged. He'd come here, on a brief visit from the twenty-first century, and he'd seen Rameses II. It was like seeing the Queen back home. He bet most ordinary Ancient Egyptians never even caught a glimpse of the Pharaoh in their entire lives.

He hurried on with new energy. King

Tut's tomb was just over that rise.

'Oh no,' groaned Finn. He dropped behind a rock. He couldn't believe it. He was so close to his goal. But there were the Medjay, sealing up the tomb again.

What am I going to do now? thought Finn in despair.

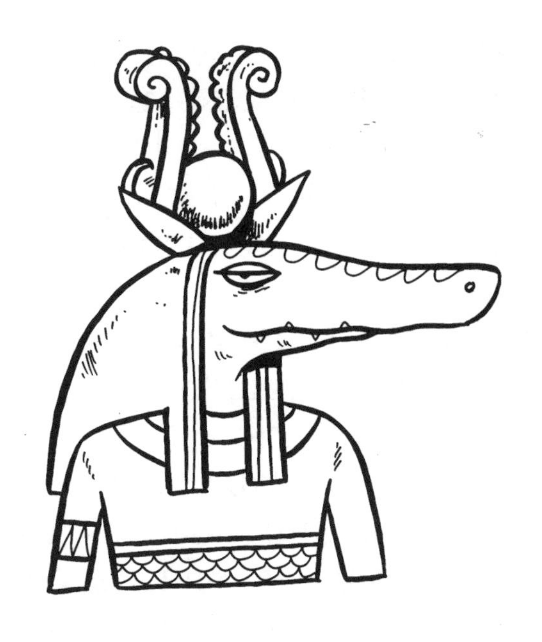

CHAPTER FIFTEEN

Finn crouched behind a rock, watching the Medjay block up King Tutankhamun's tomb so no more robbers could get in. It looked like a makeshift job. Tomorrow the tomb builders would do it properly. But it was good enough to keep Finn out. There was no way he could shift all that rubble on his own.

There was still a gap left. He had to get in there fast, before they'd finished the job. But there were four of them, far too many to sneak past. And he daren't let them see him. What if they caught him with the golden toilet? The terrible penalty for tomb-robbing sneaked into his mind again, made him squirm.

'What am I going to do?' agonized Finn again. He couldn't believe his bad luck. He was so close to being home—he could practically smell that pizza cooking. The Superloo was just metres away. Yet as far as Finn was concerned, it might have been on the moon.

One lonely little idea came into his head. He scoffed at himself, 'Don't be stupid.' But he was desperate. What else was left? He rummaged in his bag. He'd given all his charms to Karo after the crocodile incident. But he had one left.

'Oh no,' groaned Finn. 'It's a scarab!' Was his last hope really a dung beetle? He almost didn't bother. Where was Pussikins? She'd have taken those Medjay on. But there was still no sign of Gran's ferocious moggy.

Finn grasped the scarab tight. It was made of cool, green, polished stone. It was comforting somehow to feel it clenched in his fist. He screwed his eyes tight shut. 'OK, you scarab,' he muttered, as if throwing out a challenge. 'If you're supposed to be so powerful, get me home.'

He chanted it over and over again, 'Get me home, get me home.' He was wishing with all his might—he'd never wanted anything so much in his life. And he clutched that scarab so hard his knuckles turned white as bone.

At last, Finn opened his eyes, and he was just thinking, *You prat, do you really think a beetle's got some kind of magical powers?* when a gust of wind ruffled his head cloth.

Another stronger blast made the sand ripple. It grew darker; a haze hid the sun. Then, right before his eyes, something writhed up from the desert floor. It looked like a rearing cobra, but it was made of sand. It grew bigger, into a mini-cyclone, and began to travel towards the tomb.

At first, the Medjay didn't see it. It was towering now, a spinning column of sand, twisting right up into the sky.

They turned at last, alerted by the rushing noise. They barely had time to scream before it engulfed them. They ran out, trying to escape; it followed them. Now they were trapped in a roaring, swirling sandstorm. Finn watched them staggering towards the mountain track. The stinging sand twister kept pace, coiling about them, keeping them at its core, until both it and they vanished over the mountain.

The roaring sound grew faint, the wind died, the valley was peaceful again. Finn gazed after them, awestruck. But then his brain booted him into action. 'Move!' it ordered. 'They might be back any minute.' He didn't know how long that sandstorm would keep them prisoner.

He ran towards the tomb, frantically pulling at the rubble, hurling rocks aside, scraping his hands, making them bleed. But now the hole was big enough for him to squeeze through. He thrust his bag in first, dived after it, raced down the sloping tunnel. Good, they'd left the hole in the anteroom door. He dumped the toilet through, wriggled after it, landed in a clutter of bows and arrows. But he was back!

He shouted out, 'It's me! I've got King Tut's Golden Toilet Seat! Is Pussikins here yet?'

There was no answer. His own voice rang spookily round the anteroom, faded, then the deep, deep silence returned. The only light was a few feeble rays creeping in from outside. Most of the anteroom was plunged in darkness, with a glitter here and there of something gold.

'Oh no.' Finn fell to his knees. Why had he trusted that Superloo? Believed all its promises not to abandon him? It had gone back to the twenty-first century without him!

Finn sunk his head in his hands. All the fight had gone out of him. He heard scraping noises outside. Was that the Medjay coming back to finish their job? He had a choice. Give himself up to the Medjay and meet a tomb-robber's fate. Or be trapped in this grave forever with the mummy of a dead king for company.

What a choice. Since this journey

began he'd been faced with one hard decision after another. But this one seemed impossible. And he couldn't even ask his lucky scarab to help him because he'd dropped it in the sand outside.

'Stupid, stupid,' Finn muttered to himself. Slowly, shakily, he staggered to his feet. Then, *click,* light filled the tomb. Lit up every corner, dazzled him at first. A silver wall glittered, slid open, to show a toilet bowl and a jumbo bog-roll holder. Finn had never been so pleased to see anything in his life. 'You waited!' he cried.

'Of course I waited,' snapped the Superloo irritably. 'Get in, we haven't much time. I've got barely enough power to get back.'

'But what about Pussikins . . .?' Finn started to say. When suddenly behind him the wall seemed to explode. Rocks clattered into the anteroom. A fist came through, then a scarred head. It was the priest!

Finn rushed for the open Superloo door, had just hurled his bag in first, when the priest grabbed him. Finn saw mean, smouldering eyes, felt hot breath. Scar-head was horribly strong. With a cry of rage, he chucked Finn aside like a piece of rubbish. Finn, sprawled among the tangle of chariot wheels, was fighting his way out as the priest leapt into the Superloo to grab the golden toilet. The Superloo door slid shut. The 'BUSY' sign flashed up, to show there was someone inside.

'No!' cried Finn. 'You've got the wrong person!' But why should the Superloo care which human being it took back? So long as it had its precious toilet ancestor on board.

Finn heard whirring sounds. *That's the engine starting up,* he thought, panic-stricken. Now the Superloo was starting to shake. Finn was right—any second now it would whisk away, back to the twenty-first century with the priest instead of him.

But it stayed just where it was.

Finn crept closer. He reached out, touched the shiny metal. It was still here all right; it wasn't an illusion. And what were those strange gurgling sounds from inside?

Suddenly, the sign changed. Now it said 'CLEANING'.

And Finn started to laugh in hysterical relief. He just couldn't stop himself. From inside came strangled Ancient Egyptian shouts as Superloo went through its cleaning cycle: the fierce water jets, the disinfecting. Then the great silver pod rocked faster, harder. And Finn heard that rushing noise, like a giant hairdryer.

'There go the hot-air blasts!' Finn chortled merrily. 'He won't like those up his kilt!'

But the door was sliding open. Finn suddenly stopped laughing, leapt back—that priest might still be dangerous. But no chance. He came staggering out of the cubicle.

And, instead of running away, Finn found himself shrieking and pointing. 'Your tunic . . . your . . .!' But he just couldn't finish. He collapsed in a helplessly giggling heap.

The priest's linen tunic had shrunk until it looked like he'd crammed himself into a little girl's dress. It was bursting at the seams. And if his underpants had shrunk as much too, that would account for the look of pain on his face. And the way he was walking.

'Your leopard skin.' shrieked Finn, collapsing again.

Instead of fearsome, silky-smooth leopard fur, the cloak had fuzzed up. It was all fluffy now, so it looked like the priest was wearing a teddy-bear costume.

As the priest hobbled past, in gusts of piney-fresh scent, Finn was beating the floor, hugging his belly, laughing so much he couldn't even talk. Scar-head, with the same dazed expression on his face as Hoodie Boy, hauled himself out through the hole in the anteroom wall. Finn could hear the *slap, slap* of his sandals as he ran away.

'Have you quite finished?' said the Superloo sternly to Finn.

Finn gulped back his sniggers, crammed a hand over his mouth. 'Sorry, sorry.'

'I didn't do that just for your amusement,' lectured Superloo, in its toffee-nosed tones. 'It has depleted my energy supplies even further.'

'Sorry,' said Finn, sucking in his cheeks, then putting a solemn look on his face. 'It was great the way you did that,' he said to the Superloo. 'I mean, that guy was really tough.'

'Cha!' said Superloo, making its derisive snort, as if an Ancient Egyptian gangster-priest was no challenge at all.

Finn had stopped laughing now, completely. He didn't know why he'd started. He wasn't out of the woods yet. He still wasn't home. And where was Pussikins? That cat always came back. But not this time. Finn stepped inside the Superloo, checked around. Pussikins wasn't here.

'Hasn't my Gran's cat come back?' he asked Superloo again.

'No,' said the toilet. 'My sensors have not detected her. We will have to leave without her.'

'We can't,' protested Finn, horrified. 'My gran will kill me.'

'Secure the golden toilet seat,' said the Superloo in brisk, commanding tones.

Finn thought, *Where?* Frantically, he wedged his bag behind the toilet bowl.

The overhead lights in the Superloo's cubicle started to wink suddenly, on and off. They seemed to be fading.

'We must hurry,' said the Superloo. Where were its usual smug, know-it-all, tones? It even seemed a bit rattled.

'We can't leave without Pussikins,' said Finn. 'We have to wait.'

'It's now or never,' said the Superloo. 'I don't think you understand the seriousness of our situation. Do you want to be stuck in Ancient Egypt forever?'

'Wait,' said Finn as the door was sliding shut. He dashed out, grabbed his twenty-first-century clothes, shouted Pussikins one last time. No answer. He dashed back in. Then the door slid shut.

'Ready now?' asked the Superloo, with a few impatient clucks.

Finn's emotions were so mixed up: relief at going home, distress at leaving Pussikins behind, at not ever seeing Karo again; he hardly knew what he was saying.

'I never saw any pyramids!' he cried as the Superloo started spinning. He braced himself. He expected to be stuck to its metal sides like a fridge magnet as it whirled on its return journey.

But the Superloo was never predictable. Its power was dangerously low; getting back at all was touch and go. But it was determined to show Finn one last thing. It seemed to hover; its doors slid open a tiny crack. 'Look,' it said.

Finn peeped out, saw nothing but a huge, blood-red setting sun. Wind rushed by his face. Was that a bird swooping past at eye level? He looked down, *'Aaaaargh!'* They were flying high in the sky.

'The Red Pyramid at Dahshur,' announced the Superloo proudly, as if it had performed an awesome feat of navigation to give him this tiny glimpse. And it was spectacular. A great pyramid sat below them on the desert sands. It was built of pink limestone that flushed crimson in the Ancient

Egyptian sunset.

'They say,' quacked the Superloo, 'that it seems to be on fire. Does it?'

'Yes,' nodded Finn. It really does.'

'Beautiful,' sighed Superloo.

And even as Finn gazed dizzily down, clinging to the door for dear life, he was thinking, *Would you believe it?* A toilet that could appreciate beauty, that could even be poetic! He was really touched. He realized the Superloo had paused here, just for him. You can't leave Ancient Egypt, can you, without seeing at least one pyramid?

The door slid shut. 'Blast-off!' screamed the Superloo as the numbers on the digital clock started sliding. It had been reckless to make that stop. Now it had to get down to the real business of time travel.

'Ahhh!' yelled Finn as he was slammed, spread out like a starfish, on to the steel wall. His lips were dragged back, baring his teeth in a wolf-man snarl. Clothes snatched from his grasp did a mad, twirling dance together in mid-air.

For a few seconds, the world was a

silver blur then *whump,* the wall released him. He slid to the floor in a crumpled heap. Giddily, he stood up, clinging on to the giant bog-roll holder for support. After all he'd been through, he suddenly felt as weak as a newborn kitten.

'Are we home?' he asked the Superloo in a trembling voice. 'Are we *really* home?'

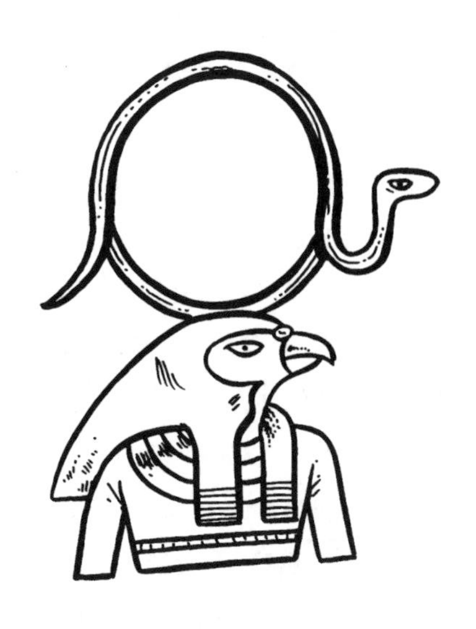

CHAPTER SIXTEEN

'Bye then,' said Finn.

'Goodbye.' The Superloo's voice was weak. The big burst of power that time travel needed had drained its energy supplies almost to zero. Finn had expected a shower of congratulations for bringing King Tut's Golden Toilet Seat back. He felt he deserved them—he'd been through a lot.

But the Superloo wasn't its usual bouncy, confident self. It seemed subdued, even a bit depressed. It didn't seem to appreciate either that Finn was going back home to a storm. When his family realized Pussikins was missing there'd be the most frightful scenes. But Finn already knew he could never tell them the truth. Who'd believe him? That she'd been left behind in Ancient Egypt? He barely believed it himself. No, he'd have to pretend he didn't have a clue where she was.

Suddenly, Finn felt desperate to be out of this claustrophobic little toilet cubicle. To breathe air that wasn't disinfected or smelling of sickly, flowery air freshener. 'Aren't you going to open the door?' he demanded.

He wasn't thirsty; he'd glugged some water from the toilet's wash-hand basin. But he was starving—he'd only had a crust of bread and a pomegranate to eat since breakfast. He was covered in bruises and scratches and so shattered he couldn't even think straight. He just wanted to get home.

'Goodbye,' said Superloo again, in a frail little voice that sounded as if it came from the bottom of a deep, deep well.

Slowly, the door slid open. Finn saw collapsing factory walls, some straggly willow trees. They were back at the Superloo's home base, its site on the disused industrial estate. Finn rushed out as if being freed from a prison cell.

'Aaaargh!' He'd just seen his reflection in the shiny metal sides. He was still wearing his Ancient Egyptian gear. He rushed back in again. 'Close the door while I change!' He tore off his head cloth, tunic and sandals, put on his own clothes.

He wondered briefly what the Superloo was going to do with King Tut's Golden Toilet. But that was its problem. Finn didn't intend to see the Superloo again, not ever. And if it tried to phone him, he'd get Mum to say, 'Finn's gone out.'

But wait a minute. There were millions of questions Finn could have asked. But one in particular swam into his mind. 'Karo's dad swapped the golden toilet for two sacks of coconuts,' he told Superloo. 'What was all that about? Coconuts for gold! Was he being ripped off?' Finn wouldn't put anything past that priest.

'On the contrary,' Superloo informed him. 'He probably got a good deal. Coconuts were a big luxury in Ancient Egypt. They had to be imported all the way from the land of Punt. Posh people would pay a fortune for them.'

'Oh, OK,' said Finn, pleased that Karo's dad hadn't been conned. If the Superloo thought this little conversation meant Finn was staying, it was wrong.

'Right,' said Finn. 'I'm *really* going now. Open this door,' he demanded. The door stayed shut.

For one heart-stopping moment, Finn thought it wasn't going to open, that the Superloo wanted to keep him prisoner, take him off on another ancient toilet quest. But then jerkily, the door opened a crack, just enough for Finn to wriggle through.

'Bye then,' said Finn. 'Thanks for the ride home.' The toilet didn't reply. Was it sulking because it hadn't got its own way? Finn already knew the great, wise Superloo had its childish side. But this time, Finn didn't care about its moods. 'Suit yourself,' he muttered.

He trudged off through a clump of tall purple weeds, climbed wearily over a pile of rubble. And there was Hoodie Boy. Just standing, waiting.

Oh no, thought Finn. *This is all I need!* He didn't have the energy left to defend himself. 'Look, I don't want no trouble,' he said hopelessly, as if he didn't think he had a choice.

'Trouble?' Hoodie Boy squinted at him. Finn caught a whiff of piney scent that still hung about him from the Superloo's cleaning cycle. He'd tried to gel down his big hair, but as Finn watched, it kept springing up into tufts. *Boing,* there went another one.

'I don't want no trouble either,' Hoodie Boy said. 'You dropped your mobile phone last night, I been trying to give it back to you.'

Finn stared at him, his mind desperately trying to do an about-turn. Hoodie Boy wasn't the menacing bully he'd imagined—he'd been trying to do Finn a favour.

Finn took the mobile. He hadn't

noticed it was missing. He carried one around like everyone else—he didn't want to be different. But it had never worked—not since his big sister sold it to him after she bought a trendier model.

'Errr, thanks,' he said to Hoodie Boy. Hoodie Boy was gazing past his shoulder. Finn thought, *Why was I scared of him?*

He could see now Hoodie Boy was tall but not hunky at all. He was weedy and gangling, like a string bean. And his face was all twitchy with anxiety as he asked, 'That toilet—that toilet . . . ?' It seemed he couldn't say any more. His experiences inside the Superloo had been too distressing. Then he blurted out, 'But it isn't there any more!'

'What?' Finn spun round. You should be able to see Superloo from here, its silver pod gleaming through the weeds. But, like Hoodie Boy said, there was nothing there. Finn rubbed his eyes, peered again. No, it had definitely gone. Maybe already off on another mission. Finn just couldn't be bothered to think about that now. He turned towards home again.

'Thanks again,' he said, slipping the phone into his pocket.

He trudged off through the wilderness, leaving Hoodie Boy gazing after him, with a deeply baffled look on his face.

Lurking behind a tree, Mr Lew Brush and his decrepit dog, Blaster, had seen the whole thing. They'd seen the Superloo suddenly materialize, as if by magic. Seen Finn rush out in his Ancient Egyptian costume, and seen Hoodie Boy and Finn meet, then leave in different directions.

'We've got some funny goings-on here,' Mr Brush murmured to Blaster.

He focused his binoculars again, right on the spot where the Superloo had been a few moments ago but now was not. It hadn't gone on a mission like Finn thought, but had retracted underground. Now there was no trace of it but its top, and that just looked like a big manhole cover. The Superloo had many features it hadn't told Finn about. Being a pop-up loo, that could disappear underground, was just one of them.

'Mmmm,' said Mr Brush. 'Fascinating.' He felt quite invigorated. Usually, he didn't like these new-fangled, hi-tech models. They had no finesse. But this one was different. They said it had a brain. And what he'd just seen seemed to bear that out. It had gone to ground, hidden itself. Did it know that the MD of Hi-Tech Toilets was trying to locate it to retrieve some kind of chip thing? And where had it been? Why was that boy dressed up in Ancient Egyptian clothes?

Mr Brush's old brain cells were whizzing around. He was a bolshy old so-and-so; he wouldn't cooperate with his boss. But the Chief Engineer was right. If you wanted someone to read the mind of a toilet, Mr Brush was your man. He was doing it now, trying to puzzle out what that toilet was up to.

But he wasn't in a hurry; he had acres of time. And oodles of patience. He didn't mind discomfort either. He was quite prepared to camp out all night if necessary. To wait until the

Superloo showed itself.

In its underground den, the Superloo had re-connected itself to its electricity supply. It was recharging fast, power flooding through all its circuits. Its superbrain was up and running. It was back to its brilliant, boastful, conniving self.

It had tapped into the computers at Hi-Tech Toilets, read all the MD's emails. It knew it was being hunted down. And it knew its very life was threatened. There was some kind of Special Task Force on the way, with the orders, 'Find and terminate!' It had covered its tracks well so far—wiped all details about itself from the Hi-Tech Toilets computers. They had no record of its exact site, or even that it was one of their pop-up models. There were other things it could do to evade capture—its superbrain could think up lots of tricks. If it was careful, cautious, it should be able to stay one step ahead of the hunters.

But the trouble was the Superloo had a weakness, a sort of Achilles heel. It was already surfing the Net and it had found another ancient toilet that needed rescuing. Where its toilet relatives were concerned it got reckless, threw all caution to the wind.

Its cubicle lights flashed on and off. *Wow, brilliant!* it thought. If it had been a little kid, it would have been dancing about with excitement. It had only just got back from Ancient Egypt. But, 'I can feel another mission coming on!' it told itself, its circuits tingling with delight.

And besides that, the Superloo was surprised to find itself missing Finn. It was thrilled to have found a toilet ancestor. But it had to admit that King Tut's Golden Toilet wasn't much company. It was at such a primitive stage of loo evolution that it hadn't even got a brain yet. One day, the Superloo would find another intelligent, highly evolved toilet to talk to. But until then it had to make do with humans.

'Now where,' it quacked to itself fussily, searching its data banks, 'did I file Finn's phone number?'

So what happened to Pussikins?

She became the favourite pet of Rameses II. She didn't miss the twenty-first century one bit. She was having the time of her life, being treated like royalty and helping the young pharaoh hunt crocs and hippos.

And what about Karo?

Karo didn't follow his dad into tomb building. He got his dream job, fishing on the Nile. He always kept the model boat—it reminded him of his foreign friend. He did miss him. But what a strange boy he'd been! Where had he come from? Where was he now? And why, oh why, had he worn his underpants on his head?